A WORLD AWAY

A World Away

GLOBAL SHORT STORIES OF LIGHT AND SHADE FROM A TO Z

Ian Cochrane

Ingramspark

Contents

About this book and author   1

Praise for the author   2

1 ABOUT MISSING PIECES – Picardy, France, 2014   4

2 AESOP IN THE BIG APPLE – New York, USA, 2015   9

3 ALL THAT GLITTERS – Helsinki, Finland, 2016   12

4 ANOTHER ODD WAR – Pretoria, South Africa, 2015   14

5 THE ART OF MUSIC – Essaouira, Morocco, 2015   16

6 THE BEAT GOES ON – New York, USA, 2013   18

7 BELLS AND WHISTLES – Tuscany, Italy, 2013   21

8 BETWEEN A ROCK AND A MONGOL
ARMY – Jeju, Korea, 2015   26

9 BROKEN BONE AND RUST – Berlin,
Germany, 2015   28

10 CHILDREN OF EARTH AND SUN –
USA, 2015   30

11 CLARISSE OF ARABIA – Helsinki,
Finland, 2015   36

12 COLD WINDS AND CORMORANTS –
Lofoten, Norway, 2015   41

13 CORNERSTONES – Lagos, Nigeria,
2015   43

14 DEMONS, GHOSTS AND GHOULS –
Norway, 2014   45

15 EFFIE AND JIMMY – Chefchaouen,
Morocco, 2015   50

16 ESCAPING THE BAKING – Kalaw,
Myanmar, 2015   52

17 FADING PHANTOMS – Dili, East
Timor, 2013   54

18 FINDING RAJ – Varanasi, India, 2016   59

19 THE FLOWER GIRL AND THE
LIZARD KING – Paris, France, 2015   61

20 FROM THE MOUTHS OF SAINTS – Normandy, France, 2016 — 66

21 GAUDI ON SUNDAY – Barcelona, Spain, 2015 — 69

22 GHOST TRAILS – Machu Picchu, Peru, 2015 — 75

23 GHOSTS IN MURK AND MIST – Venice, Italy, 2010 — 77

24 GOLDEN ORBS – Inle Lake, Myanmar, 2015 — 82

25 HAPPY NEW YEAR FRANK – New York, USA, 2014 — 84

26 KARTHIK AND THE KILLER PARROT – Doha, Qatar, 2014 — 87

27 A LONG HAUL – Mandalay, Myanmar, 2016 — 89

28 LONGINGS AND LEFTOVERS – Farmington, USA, 2012 — 91

29 LOOKING FOR A LIFE – Lagos, Nigeria, 2016 — 94

30 LOST DOGS – Lofoten, Norway, 2014 — 97

31 LOST PEARLS AND POMEGRANATES – Andalusia, Spain, 2015 — 102

32 MANDELA DAY – Johannesburg, South
Africa, 2015 108

33 MEETING SAINT LOUISE –
Trondheim, Norway, 2013 113

34 MUSIC, MADNESS AND FAME –
Prague, Czech Republic, 2013 116

35 MY BROTHER'S KEEPER – Kolkata,
India, 2015 121

36 MYSTIC GIFTS – New York, USA, 2014 123

37 NAUGHTY BUT NICE – Punakha,
Bhutan, 2015 127

38 NEW KINGDOM, OLD KINGDOM –
Luxor, Egypt, 2017 129

39 ON A LAKE OF TEARS – Halali,
Namibia, 2015 131

40 A PILLAR IN THE STORM – Qal'a
Sim'an, Syria, 2015 133

41 THE REAL WILD WEST – Vesteralen,
Norway, 2013 135

42 RIGHTS OF RETURN – New York,
USA, 2013 140

43 ROYAL WRECKAGE – Hampi, India,
2013 144

44 RUMOURS OF WRONGDOING – Lofoten, Norway, 2012   146

45 SEEKING SHANGRI-LA – The Drakensburg, South Africa, 2014   149

46 SNOW MONKEYS AND ABSENT FRIENDS – Yudanaka, Japan, 2015   153

47 SOMETHING FROM NOTHING – Doha, Qatar, 2015   159

48 SUNSET SPIRES – Bagan, Myanmar, 2015   162

49 A TALE OF THREE CITIES – Soweto, South Africa, 2013   164

50 THE TALE OF A TWISTED CROSS – Berlin, Germany, 2013   170

51 TOPKNOTS AND TALKING STONE – Easter Island, Chile, 2013   173

52 TOUCHING THE SKY – Granada, Spain, 2013   178

53 TOWERS CASTLES AND KANE – New York, USA, 2013   183

54 TRAVELLERS LOST – Uis, Namibia, 2017   186

55 UNFINISHED BUSINESS – Normandy, France, 2018   193

56 WAITING AT THE STATION – Tokyo, Japan, 2013   197

57 WANDERING WAYS – Skeleton Coast, Namibia, 2013   199

58 WAYS OF THE WORLD – Beirut, Lebanon, 2015   205

59 WHERE THERE BE DRAGONS – Kadavu, Fiji, 2012   207

60 A WHITE CHRISTMAS IN BLACK AFRICA – Lagos, Nigeria, 2014   210

61 WINDS OF WAR – New York, USA, 2014   214

References   218

About this book and author

While there is lots of `travel' in this world-wide wander, the stories are very much focused on people, places and the human condition. The tales vary in length, a menagerie of the tall and the true, all intended to lead the reader to who knows where.

Wanderlust has lured Ian to The Americas, Europe, Asia and the South Pacific, with work taking him to India, Africa, Korea and the highlands of Papua New Guinea.

He has penned several books, including –

- Indian Summers – Mumbai and Beyond
- Everything Under the Sun – Australian Short Stories of Light and Shade from A to Z

His Australian Outback short story `A Splendid Memory' was included among the 2013 non-fiction Cowley Literary Award finalists. There have also been several travel and food features published in The Australian,

Praise for the author

"Riveting as always, simply marvellous. Wonderful writing and so descriptive, your observation of detail is superb. An awe-inspiring landscape, brought to life with your usual descriptive flair" – Marty Rubin (USA), *Nothing Profound*

"I love the poignancy" – Brenda Addie (Australia), *All the World's A Stage*

"Well written; genuine and its rawness very effective" – Sandra Tyler (USA), *The Woven Tale Press*

"I have always wondered how you manage to transcend the reader to the very spot of action with but a handful of words – I guess it is some kind of magic you do, some voodoo" – Umashankar Pandey (India), *One Grain Amongst the Storm*

"Very moving, that last paragraph gave me chills" – Kris Landt (USA), *Channeling Hippocrates*

"Thank you, dear sir, for an abundantly rich shared moment in time" – Nickey Oosthuizen (South Africa)

"Bloody terrific. You traipse selectively through the mystical, reality, without disturbing the essence of history." – Ralph Jones (Australia), *Broowaha*

"Such a terrific writer. So much emotion and heartfelt feeling" – Phil (USA), *The Regular Guy NYC*

"I love the evocative atmosphere of your writing" – Guy Thair (UK), *The Wrong Stuff*

"Beautiful!" – Annie Boreson (USA), *Annie Off the Leash*

"What a wonderful word picture you paint" – Dennis Hogson (China), *The View from Fanling*

"A lovely descriptive piece" – Robert (USA), *Mulled Vine*

"Beautiful work. Great nuance and emotion" Janene Murphy (USA), *Enlightened: Light Vs Dark*

"Well written indeed – Thanks for another wonderful piece. Very touching" – Lanthie Ransom (South Africa), *Life Cherries*

"Poignant and beautiful" – Big D (UK), *Assorted Thoughts from an Unsorted Mind*

1

ABOUT MISSING PIECES – Picardy, France, 2014

From Berlin I have flown to Paris late winter, driving north for 2-hours and overnighting in the hamlet of Behen, a classic French Chateau with stately entry paved for WW2 German tanks, towers and walls from 15th and 18th centuries, the stables once bombed by American war planes. Graceful shapes glide on a Monet pond; a pair of swans not white, but black: Australian and a long way from home. I am told the first were white, until one choked on the bread of well-meaning guests, the second dying of loneliness.

Next morning, I wander the fog-laden legacies of a world at war: one war drifting into another – now WW1 criss-crossed trenches 2m deep – rolling fields of white headstones, the dead of America and from across the British Empire. A statue atop a rocky knoll is a caribou mother crying for a missing calf: testament to the fallen of the once-country-colony of Newfoundland.

I stop in a village for lunch, hazy streets deserted but for me and one other. I nod a greeting as I pass, and he stops. A great army coat hangs on a rakish frame; back bent, baguette tucked under one arm. His head turns stiffly, grey eyes empty, then suddenly wide, peering at my pack slung over one shoulder. The question is in French. He points to my forgotten German airline tag and I shake my head, apologetic as always. "No matter," he answers in perfect English. With a forced smile, he hesitates, then asks of Berlin. He has never been, "and now it is too late" he says. I answer it is quite a city, the chequered history, the architecture, the people friendly.

There is a light of recognition in his eyes. "Ah, your accent... you are Australian, and are here of course for the graves?" I nod, and he continues. "It was the Australians that arrived here to free us... in the first war... and we know the Australians well. *Oui*, there are many of your dead here."

After the fields of graves I have seen, I wonder aloud at the number of German dead. There is an audible pause. Henri's surprised at my question. "*Oui*, but of course... many... all so young." He takes a deep breath and looks away.

Henri was once a language teacher – both German and English – now doting on his old dog and beloved horses. He lives on the edge of town, not five minutes' walk from here. It's another 10 to his horses.

"You Australians, you like your coffee, *oui*?" I am

uncomfortable at imposing, but Henri's insistent: he'd enjoy the company and tugs at my jacket sleeve. "And I of course may practice my English, *oui*?"

Henri's house is small, the old family farm now too big and empty. The curtains are heavy, the room dark and musty. He has his dog, and his younger sister drops by twice a week. She worries. He was a 14 year old in WW2, his father nursing bitter memories of another: WW1, the mustard gas, mud, blood and barbed wire: 'The Great War', a 'War to end all Wars'. Henri shakes his head, unruly fringe falling over one eyebrow.

This time the Germans took the family horses: all but one, which Henri hid in the forest and somehow visited twice a day. Later, with the war turning, there was help on the farm: a German prisoner – only 3-years older than Henri – fair hair and freckles. The soldier spoke little French, but tried; missed his Berlin home, his mother, younger brothers and sister. Henri smuggled fresh-baked bread, some beer when he could, the soldier talking of 'rats the size of dogs' on a freezing Russian front, and happier times riding on Spandau Forest paths.

Only once did Henri ask about the killing, recalling the German wiping his eyes on a frayed army sleeve. Henri coughs. With the end WW2, there was so much hate.

He lowers his eyes, shrugs and shifts in his seat. His sister told him of their father shouting, and of a fearful mother. There was a string of letters with not one reaching Henri; the German's letters burnt rather than passed on to a damaged father's only son.

The mother dies, but life goes on: the farm, what is left of the family, and Henri's horses. Years later the father dies too, Henri's sister collecting her father's things and finding one last letter in the bottom of their father's grand mahogany desk: a letter addressed to her brother; a lone letter somehow spared and forgotten for over 10yrs. His sister called Henri in from the horses.

I look across the table; a blue and white porcelain sugar bowl in the centre, the cloth of yellowing French lace. There is the baguette and strawberry jam, an empty brandy bottle on a sideboard, with a single glass. Henri coughs again, and falls silent, leans towards the sideboard, pulls something from a camphor-wood box, folded paper smudged and faded. He grasps the letter in wrinkled hand, reaches for wire-rimmed glasses that stay in his cardigan pocket, his eyes again the vaguest grey. He recalls that day so clearly, his sister leaving him alone in their dead father's study.

I see Henri sitting there, looking nervously about. He is feeling guilty, having never sat in his father's chair. He opens the letter in one hand, fumbling with his father's Meerschaum pipe in the other; the smell of his father's tobacco so strong that Henri drops the pipe, grey eyes drawn to the paper in his hand. The letter is creased and crumpled, the words in broken French, uncertain and clutching at straws.

I fiddle with my coffee cup and look across the table at Henri, now in his mid-80s and until recently, riding his favourite mare side-saddle: no doubt a sight, the now old man with his mop of hair and great grey army coat.

Henri turns the letter on its side, hand and letter trembling.

He stares at the table and has no need for the reading glasses that poke from his pocket, knowing the German's words verbatim. Henri clears his throat and sniffs. "As you see, my friend, my French has improved little, but I try. So, here I am writing in the final hope there will somehow be an answer." The breath seems to catch in Henri's chest.

There is silence and I wait until Henri finally looks up. He remembers those WW2 war years: the owls at night, the distant artillery, the young German's pained face, the smell of horses in the barn; their steaming backs after washdown, the bags of chaff, the wet turf after a summer shower, shaded forest paths. He remembers his father's erratic drinking and the horror stories of WW1: the blood and the bodies, waving red poppies in churned fields of mud. He remembers his mother's favourite tortoiseshell comb in those streaks of auburn-grey hair, the lavender smell of her alabaster skin, fresh-baked bread on a cold winter's day.

Suddenly it is late afternoon. Henri shakes his head. Yes, his mother knew, but said nothing.

The letter is on the table now, Henri's eyes empty once more. These days he passes the time juggling jigsaws, mostly pictures of Spandau and Picardy, but never seems to finish one. He rolls his eyes and shrugs. "*Oui*, there is always the piece that is missing."

2

AESOP IN THE BIG APPLE – New York, USA, 2015

A small green plaque reads `Ancient Playground', the entrance a pair of black cast-bronze gates set between tall rectangular pillars of polished pink granite; topped by bears on the left – one upright – three deer on the other. The pillars are engraved in gold letters, dedicated to a `William Church Osborn'

"PRESIDENT THE CHILDREN'S AID SOCIETY 1901-1945"

A dog walker crosses 5th Avenue, stopping by the picket fence and juggles three assorted dogs; a beagle, a Jack Russell and an errant Afghan. There is a smattering of Central Park snow. I catch here eye and ask about the `Ancient' theme.

"Oh yeah, I see what you mean. It's a European thing apparently, something from the 60s." She waves across to Egyptian pyramids with her free hand, the paths, the sand and running stream; the building materials concrete, brick and wood. "It's all about climbing, imagination and adventure. Do you know that playground rules prohibit adults unless in the company of children?"

Osborn studied law and served New York City in political and charitable tasks, although never seeking political office. But it seems this playground is not so ancient, constructed to replace the original built upon Osborn's death; the gates – a creation of sculptor Paul Manship – installed there in 1953 and considered that year's most distinguished artwork in New York City.

"Take a close look," the dog walker invites, as she again tugs at the Afghan's lead. "It's Aesop's Fables of course, see?'" And as if talking to herself: "Mmmm, not sure how many New Yorkers even know of this place." The gates are classic Art Deco, five of Aesop's ancient stories in honour of Osborn, a busy man regarded as one of New York's first citizens; somehow juggling Presidential roles with the `New York Society of the Ruptured and Crippled', along with `The Metropolitan Museum of Art'.

In his gates I recognise the familiar form of tortoise and hare, the crane and the peacock. There are the lamb and wolf; city mouse, country mouse. A fox sits on the ground, looking up at a crow in a tree, cheekily asking if the bird sings as beautiful as it looks. As the story goes, the crow is duly flattered, opening its beak to say thank you and subsequently dropping the cheese; Aesop's fables a fitting touch for a kids' playground.

My ponderings are interrupted by the helpful dog walker. "The original playground was over there you know, closed in the 70s due to work on the museum." She points to the adjacent Metropolitan Museum of Modern Art. "The Osborn gates weren't installed here until 2009." Her eyes are fixed on the gates, seemingly oblivious to the restless canine charges at our feet. "Can you imagine something so beautiful stuck in storage for 30-years?" She does not wait for an answer.

3

ALL THAT GLITTERS – Helsinki, Finland, 2016

In the cool of morning, I wrap a scarf around my neck, passing Helsinki joggers and cafes loaded with coffee- drinking, sociable, sun-loving Finns, and busy, pale- skinned girls in sensible shoes. I step aside as a cyclist in civvies and no helmet explodes from a crooked cobblestone laneway. Others weave between cars, buses, and concertina trams; the green and gold reminiscent of my far-off Melbourne home.

Waiting for my tram, I'm pondering the up-beat 'Western' manner of these Finns. Joggers on the streets? Definitely not something common over the Russian border from where I've just come.

There's the great boom of a ship's horn, the bright blue sky an odd opposite to the long drawn-out winters – bleak and black. My companion smiles, her head tilted to one side. "We must simply cope with the short days… *ja* …and the depression… it can be too much for some."

Her chatter is measured and matter-of-fact. "All that sparkles, it is not silver here, and you will see the weekend Tallinn ferry mostly full, with partying Finns Hell-bent on cheap alcohol and self-destruction."

4

ANOTHER ODD WAR – Pretoria, South Africa, 2015

I must have passed him, walked right past; his bony back propped against the mausoleum wall while taking his mid-day nap. He wears a threadbare navy-blue sweater despite the 35degC Pretoria heat. I am wandering gravel paths, by graves, headstones and monuments. Jerome has approached me, his black face more puzzled than rebuking. He looks over towards the main entry, with me having parked way outside and having crawled through a hole in the wire fence. I admit I am lost.

Jerome smiles, says nothing at first, picking at a hole in his sleeve while listening intently to my excuses, then turning and slowly heading down one of the many paths. I follow.

The summer grass smells dry and parched. He stops at a simple grave. "You have kangaroos of course, and many horses." It seems an Australian woman was here just last week. "She was also asking after your Handcock and Morant."

I am surprised, and yes, am here to find the grave of soldier-poet and drover `Breaker' Morant, but knowing nothing of `Handcock'.

"This lady, she leaves me a book you see, with a brown cover." Jerome pauses and frowns. "It has pages missing, am not so learned, and do not always understand." Jerome stoops down to straighten a wilting red poppy between two stones. I am stuck for a reply, not initially taking his point. But then I get it.

He can't see the logic in far off Australia sending troops here, to South Africa of all places, to fight South Africans in the Second Boer War. "But you are both white men. You both have the same slouch hat. And both are farmers and horsemen."

Jerome stands by my side in silence, and we both stare down at the grave: the final resting place of two Australian soldiers sharing the same tomb, having both been court-martialled by their own British allies, convicted of killing South African civilians and a German missionary, and in turn shot by British firing squad in 1902.

5

THE ART OF MUSIC – Essaouira, Morocco, 2015

We are ambling by a harbour clogged with a maze of blue fishing boats. There is fresh orange juice on the way. Sprawling nets cross our path, tended by net menders. Imad stops, talks to the menders, and I gaze across at larger boats, one unloading a catch of sardine and shark. There is swirling screeching seabirds overhead, salt and fish guts in the air... and the hypnotic strains of some string instrument from the shade and shadows of medina walls.

Imad collects his bicycle, and I peer up at a 3m mural down an adjacent brown ochre laneway, the street portrait of a musician beaming down on passing pedestrians. He is dressed in classic Moroccan garb, a flowing red djellaba and matching fez. There is a slight smile under a wispy moustache and he strums a guitar-like instrument.

My companion Imad is in his 30s – his English good – so I ask about Jimi Hendrix, Cat Stevens and Frank Zappa; all supposed to have come this way. I'd read that Hendrix wrote `Castles Made of Sand' about some collapsing castle ruins just south of here.

Imad is no help though, knows nothing of these names. "Yes, music is always everywhere here, like this painting on the wall." He shakes his shaggy head. "But me, I am an artist, and it is art that is the soul of this town."

6

THE BEAT GOES ON – New York, USA, 2013

It's New Year's Day, and Joe Strummer – poet of the streets – looks down from a giant mural facing Tompkins Park. From here I walk west with my girlfriend towards St Marks church-in-the-Bowery, past webs of winding fire escapes; hands deep in our pockets, wrapped scarves covering chilled cheeks and chins. Tribal drums sound from subway stairs – reminiscent of Sudan, Nigeria or maybe Marrakesh. Steam rises from underground labyrinths through metal manhole covers in the middle of the road.

Finally, the shape of the church looms between boughs of bare winter trees, small burial ground to one side, mounds and tacit tottering headstones, the traffic-laden Bowery on the other; a simple Romanesque forum of a place, gable front facade atop high colonnades.

We're at the 39th Marathon Benefit Reading, an annual celebration of the spoken word. Today's programme has almost 200-names of poets, writers, performers and musicians. There are those I know of, including Lee Ranaldo and Suzanne Vega; and those I now know. Out back there's pizza, beer, wine and conversation; sure-fire poet fodder. In the main we're an older crowd, arriving in dribs and drabs, small groups gathering at the door. Inside is a large rectangular hall, steps rising to a low carpeted stage and central wooden podium. The steps extend down both sides to the back, the ceiling a high arched space; columned portico balcony both sides and rear. Two rows of south-facing stained glass soak up the last of the winter sun – unspoken glowing stories in blues and reds – traditional themes below and abstract above; a melding of the old and new.

We sit at the back, looking across a sea of heads; an eclectic crowd on rows of seats and raised and carpeted side-wall steps. There're mops of wild hair – much of it grey – beards, bald pates and pony tails; and there's a menagerie of New York winter headwear; Baltic sailors' caps, berets, Tam O'Shanters, Inca tea cosies, beanies and peaked. A sound man wears a bear-head hat.

But the young are here too. At the podium a poet holds her little daughter's hand, the toddler staring distractedly into the crowd while her mother reads, causing smiles and snickers and stealing the show. A young girl sits close by, maybe 17, chin sitting on the thick roll of a woollen sweater, legs in tight blue denim; rolling a biro in her fingers in between scribbles on a small notepad. A guy in his 20s fiddles with the sleeve of his Afghan coat and chews on his lip as he takes notes on his iPhone.

One poet heads up the steps with something akin to a skip and an excited jump, arriving with a mischievous cackle at the podium. Born with cerebral palsy, Jennifer Bartlett is a self-described `boring white girl'. She strikes me as a driven woman with a cheeky bent, writing on the human condition; how people do and don't fit together. Her eyes are bright as she offers a question. "Is it true the crippled are closer to enlightenment?"

Iconic New York poet Patti Smith appears; an unscheduled visitor prevented from travelling due to some passport issue. "Where better to spend a New Year's Day?" she asks. "I'm hoping for a better 2013 though. It's been tough this year, with the fury of Mother Nature, God Bless her, and more recently Human nature." There is a collective sigh at her reference to the floods and the recent Connecticut mass shooting.

The musician Steve Earle talks of the spirit within these walls, honoured to be `breathing the same hallowed air' as `real poets', present and past. I look around me and see the blurred faces of the 40s and 50s, the Beat poets of that time, Burroughs, Cassady, Corso, Ferlinghetti and Ginsberg; Johnson, Kerouac, Kyger and Snyder. I feel the need for change, the humour, mirth, the tragedy and pathos; the beat of this village they call New York.

7

BELLS AND WHISTLES – Tuscany, Italy, 2013

Dragano is an editor initially from up north. He is tall and rakish, the wisp of a moustache and sleek brown hair; has the habit of whistling unexpectedly, as he ponders the ways of an unjust world while stroking a precocious black cat. His villa is classic Tuscan, the bricks and terra cotta gables more orange than red. I soak up the sun while a younger woman serves coffee and biscotti, rubs Dragano's shoulder and returns to the kitchen.

I mention Venice: Dragano's birthplace and from where I have come. "Ah yes, but that was not to be." He smiles wistfully and his eyes drift off to one side. "It is of course, a woman that brings me here." There's a shake of his head and he seems happy to change the subject. "So," he fixes me in his gaze, "you are on your way to San Gimignano? It is but one hour from here, and they have the best artisans."

Dragano squints in the sunlight and leans forward in his chair. "My son is such a craftsman." He stares at the paving at his feet, and the sound of schoolkids drifts in from the street. "It is from his mother he gets this gift. In early days she is wild and free; these days a teacher of art." His eyes meet mine and there is a fleeting smile. An odd silence permeates the courtyard until a low melodic whistle escapes from his lips. I note his son's name and enter it in my phone.

Next morning, I park in the shadow of 13th century walls, entering the town via the Porta San Giovanni, lingering awhile in the town square by the bell tower; this bell one of many that apparently rang of their own accord in 1253 upon the death of the town's paralysed patron saint. Crooked cobbled steps climb ancient laneways to the highest knoll where I sit in a balmy breeze. A brick and stone arbour is part-gnarled wisteria; sprouts of mauve framing a Tuscan montage of rolling hills beyond. I turn and stare across merchant house-towers that soar to a height of 50m and once numbered seventy-two in all, built by jealous feudal families craving wealth and influence.

I breathe in the scent of warm rock and earth, brushing frazzled tufts of summer grass from jeans and boots. I pick up my pack and check my phone. On a meandering staircase I stop to ask and confirm the name. "*Si Signor*, the bellmaker? But of course, but that is not the family name." I am directed to take another turn and yet another set of stairs further down the hill, to a rustic Tuscan shopfront; the head of the window a low Roman arch. I stand outside, peering through glass ancient and unclear.

The door is heavy, the handle a dull brass ring. I twist and push the door ajar. There's the sound of someone whistling from somewhere within. The single room is all clutter, the now silent occupant still unseen. I push past a bench and register, entering a Lewis Carroll wonderland.

A chorus of tinkling bells ring in the breeze, the draft from the street having followed me in. The door swings shut with a bang, and I jump. A mosaic lamp flares into life, throwing mirror-ball beams about the scene: this maze of fairy bells that swing higgledy-piggledy in their web of gossamer threads and tiny shards of Venetian glass. More bells hang from timber-boarded, odd angled-ceilings and crooked metal brackets perched on walls of weathered brick, each adorned with delicate hues; sprays of flowers and cats in tuxedos. There is a 60s ambience of Nag Champa incense and wet clay.

I am startled by a voice from a back corner. "*Si*, the cats; they are my favourites. You will be taking something?" He sits on a stool, behind potters' wheel and work bench; piles of pieces midway between paintbrush and wheel. The voice is husky, his father's brown hair parted at the side; the same tilt of his head and sharp nose. But the voice has an awkward disconnect; each word fighting to finish a sentence; and yet he can certainly hold a tune.

There is a shuffle and now he is half standing. He is shorter than his father, or maybe just slightly bent. His movement is awkward when he turns to follow my finger pointing across the room, but there are so many to choose from. I finally decide on a single bell hanging against the wall. He shuffles towards me, laughing wildly at my indecision until he gasps for air. "This is the one?" he finally blurts out.

He's somehow thrown himself past me, long rod in hand, lunging and leaning with awkward gait. I am even more un-comfortable now, seeing the extent of his physical difficulty and making things worse by offering help. His body twists, his face a picture of concentration; his tongue poking from the corner of his mouth and eyes screwed up. "No, no... this, is something I must do." He extends the rod into the clutter and I hold my breath, fearing he'll bring the whole lot down about our ears.

Dragging his right arm by his side, his right foot too seems a burden; and yet he deftly turns the rod side-on, catching the bell's delicate hanging thread and releasing it from its wall-mounted bracket. There is a burst of laughter when he spies me frozen as I stare; him wielding a shepherds' crook to capture his tiny pottery bells daubed with feline friends, in splashes of black; the flowers of lemon and fairy blue.

He props on a stool behind the register, and I ask him how he put all this together. "Oh, my mother, she helps me." He battles on wrapping my bell in green crepe paper. "I owe her much," he says. "She raises me alone." I fidget with my pack and look away. "No, I do not remember my father," he continues, his head jerking to one side. "He died when I was so young." I am puzzled but say nothing. He is sharp this young man, and I feel his eyes sizing me up. "Things are hard for her I think...with me of course." He falls quiet, the grey eyes lowered, his tongue again in the corner of his mouth as he battles the wrapping paper.

One month later, I unexpectedly find myself back in Florence. "You are back so soon my friend?" Dragano asks, and we sit once more in the same courtyard exchanging idle chatter on literature, politics and the likelihood of me receiving a Florence traffic infringement notice when eventually returning home to Melbourne.

I am fumbling with a small painted bell in my jacket pocket, Dragano's stare intense. "Ah, so you met?" he inquires with apparent surprise. I answer yes, but that his son was difficult to find. I show my friend the bell, turn it between my fingers and place it back in the green crepe wrapping. Dragano's eyes narrow and he hesitates. "And you spoke?" I reply that the shop was busy, and there was little chance. My friend's eyes soften and wander across to the dark-haired young woman busying herself with dinner at the kitchen window.

I am thinking of a young Italian couple; the ecstatic announcement of a new pregnancy, the arrival of a beautiful new baby boy, and the concern of a doctor for a toddler that walks with a slight sway and seems to favour one side over the other. I see the years that follow, the dwindling time the young couple have for each other; the unravelling of lives, the widening gap and the tortured priorities of two people struggling with blame and the allocation of affection.

8

BETWEEN A ROCK AND A MONGOL ARMY – Jeju, Korea, 2015

The railings are wood, the Korean wind cold, a pine forest path perched on 30m cliffs. I'm 2km west of Seogwipo, on the craggy, crater-pocked southern island of Jeju: the rock just offshore on rolling seas; a 20m basalt pillar, ancient, volcanic, geyser-lava-wrought. I'm surrounded by coated, fur-collared tourists, families, parents – grand and great. Cameras click and whirr: honeymooner and schoolkid selfies in mid-winter sun; laughter and light-hearted banter.

But there's the wail of wind in the pines, the timeless rush of surf on rocks: Jeju's history a troubled one. From

1231 to 1259, Korea is a battleground when a courageous Korean soldier dresses this rock as a giant Korean general; an entire Mongol army driven to suicide rather than face such a demon.

9

BROKEN BONE AND RUST – Berlin, Germany, 2015

Daniel Libeskind's design is the winner of a competition in 1989 – the same year the Berlin Wall comes down – this his radical zigzag, windowless design resembling a shattered Star of David. I'm standing a little shell-shocked, in the basement of this ultra-modern complex opened in 2001, me having wandered this edgy, arty city of World Wars, Cold Wars and even colder memories.

I turn a corner on a downward bound concrete ramp, this narrow canyoned path called the `Memory Void', and leading another 50m ahead, to end with the deadest of ends. I stare down beside me in utter silence, at a sunken flowerbed on my left, the dishevelled stacks of 10,000 faces: piles of rusted steel plates a bed of steel discs, little and large, each with eyes wide and howling mouths. Noses are fearful and narrow. This is Menashe Kadishman's installation `Shalekhet', meaning `Fallen Leaves'.

I shiver, my breathing frozen in this oddly cold void, until my thoughts are fractured by kids chatting behind me, then footsteps as they run and jump up and on the mass of faces. The kids run headlong on, and past me, black sneakers on rusted steel, their echoes the crunch of breaking bones.

10

CHILDREN OF EARTH AND SUN – USA, 2015

The sound of our footsteps is muffled by patchwork drifts of snow on a gravel track winding past the bottom of carpark stairs. Surrounding hills are covered in local rhododendron; the air icy, the trees tall, rough barked and bare. Our guide strides ahead – rugged-up for the 10min walk – black puffer coat full length, fur trim sleeves and hood. She stops, adjusts her mittens and points her umbrella. There's a gap in the trees, and the house appears on cue among flurries of snow-flakes that float to rest on a leaf-littered forest floor.

Brenda is a local, and long-time disciple of the American architect Frank Lloyd Wright. And we are at Fallingwater, Wright's iconic creation, 70km southeast of Pittsburgh and now a monument to the architect's base philosophy, `Usonian' design, organic architecture in harmony with humanity and the environment. US architects voted this house the 'best all-time work of American architecture'.

From a southern Melbourne summer, I have flown to NYC with my girlfriend, our aim to first see Wright's Guggenheim Museum. From the beginning of 5th Avenue we've ambled northwards through city environs reminiscent of Paris, along an avenue part Gothic and part Renaissance before morphing into a New York that Wright called '...an affected riot' and a `...monument to the power of money and greed...'; then finally onwards to the Guggenheim which opened the year of Wright's death.

A Chinese tour group bursts from the museum door, chattering and juggling cameras, neat casual gear, flag bearer up front; above us Wright's spiralling, white tiered, wedding-cake design, between the affluence of Upper Eastside apartments

Turning my gaze across 5th Avenue I've admired the simple wilds of Central Park; its brooding blanket of fine powder snow and the bones of bereft trees. A squirrel jumps and props at the kerb, red-grey tail arched above the white.

Finally, at Fallingwater we are now standing on the causeway bridge, Brenda, my girlfriend and I, Bear Run stream gurgling below us, the house a series of miraculously cantilevered concrete tiers over rocky outcrops and white water.

Brenda says the waterfall had always been a focal point of the owners' life here, the Kaufmans originally owning a rustic weekender and their son a student of Wright's. "But they were unprepared for Wright's insistence on the importance of the falls; telling the Kaufmans to live with the water and not just admire it. His grand plan included the forest, the rock ledges and boulders."

We round the corner of the house and I search for an entry, an opening in the rock wall off to the side; hardly a main entrance I am thinking. Brenda smiles. She has heard it all before. "Ah, yes, there are surprises here."

Brenda waits as we hang our coats inside. Narrow stairs and passages meander cave-like and indicative of Wright's approach; thick walls of local sandstone. In the living room, a giant boulder is part of the hearth, the ceilings low; my eyes drawn to the winter wilderness outside. The windows are clear, mitred glass with no cornice or frames to obstruct the view.

From the centre of the room Brenda waves a hand towards horizontal sliding panels of glass; an enclosed stairwell leading down to the babbling stream below. "The panels of course are sliding, and can be opened in summer to admit water- cooled breezes." It takes me a moment to absorb the significance of Wright's radical 1939 design, and I find it difficult to imagine such an innovative architect with little work when commissioned by the Kaufmans to design this place. But Wright's life was anything but ordinary.

Even before Wright's birth in 1867, his mother declared her son would "grow up to build beautiful buildings." The young Wright himself would claim he would "be the greatest architect of all time". His first marriage at 21yrs old, to Catherine Tobin, gave him the social connections he needed.

As a Chicago architect there was some success blending buildings with landscape, before his designs became more experimental. By 1907 he was challenging the moral majority with his long hair, broad-brimmed hats, red-lined cape and cane. There were also joyrides with married women in his luxurious open car; his exploits culminating with Wright leaving for Europe with Mamah Cheney, a client's wife. He left his practice, his six and her two children behind.

Wright would return to build Taliesin in the Wisconsin wilderness, a melding of his organic theories and an isolated citadel to ride out the public storm with Cheney. With his fall from favour, there would be few commissions for 20-years.

Worse was yet to come, with Wright taking 10yrs to recover from the personal devastation that followed. While working at his Chicago office in 1914, now age 47, a servant bolted doors and poured petrol on the floor of Taliesin, attacking the occupants inside with an axe and hunting down those trying to escape. Taliesin was razed to the ground, with seven murdered including Cheney and her two children.

Wright buried Cheney in a simple grave and began work on Taliesin 2. Sailing to Japan in 1916 with the bohemian clairvoyant Mariam Noel, he opened an office in Tokyo. With Wright's divorce from his first wife he entered into a volatile marriage with Noel, only to see it disintegrate with her opium addiction.

Next Wright met Montenegrin dancer Olgivanna Milanoff in 1924 at the Petrograd Ballet in Chicago. While dealing with a messy divorce from Noel, Wright saw yet another fire; this time destroying Taliesin 2. Wright again rebuilt and re-married, only to suffer a bout of pneumonia. It was Milanoff who convinced Wright to finally leave Wisconsin for the sun and pure air of Arizona.

With Milanoff, Wright's luck improved; the architect appearing on the cover of Time magazine. From here until his death, Wright was a celebrity of radio, film and TV; although labelling the latter `chewing gum for the eyes'. Fallingwater was completed in 1939, followed by Taliesin West: becoming his Arizona home and architectural studio.

We have completed Brenda's Fallingwater tour, standing by a low bench at a bend downstream and peering back to the house; through a silent forest, now bathed in weak streaks of sun and flurries of winter snow. We exchange glances; my girlfriend an aspiring architecture student in earlier times. Does it live up to expectations I wonder?

I see the house as a transported Shinto vision of rural splendour; Bear Run stream tumbling and winding towards us from beneath Wright's radically-cantilevered terraces that seem to float ten metres above the gurgle and rush of the water gods.

We are pondering the lot of Wright, dying in 1959 and his ashes now in far-off Arizona at Taliesin West; interred alongside those of his last wife Milanoff, at the headquarters of the Frank Lloyd Wright Foundation. We exchange glances, and my girlfriend coughs. "You know... I suppose I could understand Wright's broken heart lying among the charred ruins of Taliesin 1, a tragedy that would probably have wrecked a normal person, but really... I think his heart is here."

We both fall silent and gaze about us; the wet forest

sentinels, the damp rolling hills, the hypnotic serenity of Fallingwater. I am thinking, yes, the whole place is the epitome of the man's philosophy: `Buildings, too, are children of Earth and Sun'.

11

CLARISSE OF ARABIA – Helsinki, Finland, 2015

Outside the station I squint in late summer sun, a grand entrance clad in grey Finnish granite and guarded by lamp-holding titans: stern-faced stone men far too serious to be the animated rap stars of railway advertising campaigns. At their feet, there is a kid busker with peaked cap and grandmother's clarinet.

With a population of five million, I am in an often-forgotten land of modern innovation, Nokia and the birthplace of the mobile phone. Welcome to Helsinki, late 2012: home to global business powerhouses Kone, Iitala, Marimekko and Fiskars, and this year's World Design Capital.

After dinner I relax at the hotel, the talkative barman

curious. "You are visiting Arabia?" He talks up the merits of good design and working hard. I see the irony of a small country, successful in a competitive world; where kids start compulsory education a year later than most in the Western world and are not academically measured for the first 6-years of schooling. When offering some credit to the government, I am greeted with a narrow-lipped smile and reminded where I am. "You are at this moment in Finland, and the power here, it is in the will of ordinary people." I'm suitably rebuked. "Government should not be relied upon for such innovation." He pours me another beer. "For example, here it is our Society for Crafts and Design that is founded way back in 1875... by ordinary people."

In the cool of morning, I wrap a scarf around my neck, passing joggers and cafes loaded with coffee-drinking, sociable, sun-loving Finns, and busy, pale-skinned girls in sensible shoes. I step aside as a cyclist in civvies and no helmet explodes from a crooked cobblestone laneway. Others weave between cars, buses, and concertina trams; the green and gold reminiscent of my Melbourne home. I have been told to take the No 8 from Apollonkatu across city, and then north to meet Clarisse at Arabia.

The tram hums, steel wheels on shining rails, the carriage empty but for two gangly teenagers up front, each absorbed with mobile phones, blue jean legs splayed across the aisle; backpacks piled on seats of the plushest red. Avenues are wide, the traffic and people thinning. There is a roundabout, a rocky knoll of a park, patchy grass and chip bark, trees exploding green.

Fleeting tram stops are raised islands, a one-way road either side. A central median strip has tall power pylons; steel tower skeletons that flicker, crossings come and go. Kids' playgrounds sit on odd-shaped corners, deserted now, past patrons at schools and kindergartens, toys stranded on forlorn fields: Lilliput dolls' houses scattered about, trucks and tractors in ragtag Nordic wagon trains. Neighbourhood apartments are austere, blockish, but Finnish and functional in colours brown, grey or cream.

It is 20-minutes before I get there, where Helsinki was founded in 1550, the tram in an arc, grinding to a stop on a grand stone plaza. At a set of glass doors, I turn and look past the tram, across the plaza to wide concrete steps rising to a paved patio over a hidden underground carpark. I am standing in the shadow of a tall rectangular glass building; an adjacent brick tower with large letters rising vertically upwards: `ARABIA'. I am in the right place after all. Glass doors open behind me and I turn to meet Clarisse.

"Ah yes, of course; the name." Clarisse chuckles. "As with most things Finnish, there is a simple answer." She waves an arm from left to right. "This was once the site of the old industrial area, from back in 1873: the biggest ceramics factory in all of Europe." Clarisse gazes across the plaza. The tram heads back to the city. "It was thought to be so far from the modern centre that they called it `Arabia'."

Through the glass doors Clarisse peers about. "But now, as you see, this is a factory no longer. Today we have houses of design, the home of the famous Marimekko of course. There is a library and departments of learning: Applied Sciences, Arts, Design and Music."

We sit at a small square table with sparing lines. Clarisse looks down at a short black espresso and tilts her head. "And yes of course, we have restaurants, and good coffee." Students roam in loose groups, mixes of male and female. They chat in English, one with a Rasta hat, over-sized, floppy and lop-sided; another a tie-dye scarf tossed over one shoulder and almost to the ground. A girl has a laptop tucked under one arm and tugs at the sleeve of a cashmere sweater while balancing a mobile between shoulder and neck. I could be in Melbourne, London or San Francisco.

Away from the Design Houses, we walk well-tended lawns, by pocket plots of fruit and vegetables. There is a lake, a bicycle path and a gaggle of Toulouse geese. Sculptures and murals sit on corners and walls. Clarisse looks puzzled. "Yes… but of course there is art here; a world is nothing without art. And art must be in each place of living. The developers here, they must always spend something on art pieces. And this is why we see art in the streets and the courtyards; murals on the buildings." I am taken aback by the scale of the project. Clarisse smiles and tosses her head. "Yes, yes; I know what you are thinking. It is all so new, a large area, and yet these days so close to the city." I nod. "Well, yes, there have been great changes here. Before 2000, this place was better known for its homeless."

Waiting for the tram, I'm still pondering the up-beat `Western' manner of these Finns. Joggers in the streets? Definitely not something common over the Russian border from where I have just come. "You think so?" Clarisse's face is beaming, her clearly impressed, before screwing up her eyes in concentration. "But we Finns must also live in the real world. Our winters too, are long."

"So mostly, we cope with the short days... and the depression... it can be too much for some." Clarisse's chatter is matter-of-fact. "All that sparkles, it is not silver here, and you will see the weekend Tallinn ferry mostly full, with partying Finns Hell-bent on cheap alcohol and self-destruction." Clarisse falls quiet for a moment. "Sometimes there can be emptiness." She shakes her head. "Hard working? Yes, I suppose it is true. But of something I am very sure, it must not be only about the work. We must allow children the time to be children; and we must surely teach all children music and art for a happy life."

12

COLD WINDS AND CORMORANTS – Lofoten, Norway, 2015

The Norwegian ferry approaches, an Arctic wind loaded with the smell of salt and wooden racks of sun-dried cod. I dally by the terminal, peering through jetty cracks to the heaving black below, then gazing out to a wine-dark sea.

Three silent cormorants sit on a nearby skerry, wet wings extended out to dry, long snakelike necks and hooked beaks held high. These must surely be THE three cormorants of Rost, an ancient tale of bird brothers in a magical land south of Skomvaer, where drowned sailors live forever and visit grieving families in the form of cormorants.

13

CORNERSTONES – Lagos, Nigeria, 2015

It is the wet season, the smells fresh and green, this Lagos urban road a full-blown lake. I am in this most affluent of Lagos suburbs, the street kerb broken wherever there is one. The sky is heavy with the still gloom of pending rain. Tumbled-down, lean-to shops line tall block walls topped with rolls of razor wire, overgrown vacant lots, owned by someone no doubt. These are the same family shops the council would force elsewhere, to `tidy' the place and encourage permanent buildings, and the accompanying rents that will be due.

There is a battered white van on a precarious angle. That is the suburban shuttle with grill and bumper submerged, the suspension shot. A broken, black Mercedes has two wheels hanging over a metre-deep gutter; the gutter a playground for local barelegged kids.

Blessing stands off to the side, turning her head this way and that as if surveying the best route across the flooded obstacle course. She stands tall and straight, but I don't know how. I have noticed her before, in one of the shops, and walking to and fro each day. She is often loaded up with bottles and baskets of food, a wide-eyed baby strapped to her back with a white herringbone blanket. Blessing takes lunch to her sister who sells plants by the roadside, and an uncle stricken by polio.

She sells whatever she can along the way. "It is important, I have three other children, and I must do what I can." I ask her the kid's name. Blessing coughs, and the bucket on her head shakes. "My boy? `Cornerstone' he is called."

14

DEMONS, GHOSTS AND GHOULS – Norway, 2014

Four metre waves batter our ferry on the fiercest piece of water in the world. We are 100km west of the Norwegian mainland, on the Lofoten Archipelago, and this is the Maelstrom; first mentioned by the Greeks 3000 years ago and immortalized in the iconic writings of Edgar Allen Poe and Jules Verne. But it is the artist and poet Theodor Severin Kittelsen who's the icon here, his sketches of trolls and wildlife legendary; and I wonder what could drive a man said to be lyrical, macabre, anthropomorphic, soulful and poetic. Only one day earlier a Lofoten blacksmith suggested "personal demons".

"You have heard of him?" Marius seemed surprised. "With not so much printed in the English language, I am thinking he does not receive the international attention." Marius is thinking out loud, peering intently at a newly formed cormorant glowing red between smithy's callipers. "This man, he could capture the mind and the moods... the conditions of Norwegian society and nature."

I am reminded of a sketch lying flat in the grey pressed-metal cabinet of an Oslo museum: an ancient crone with bent back shuffling from house to house. This is Kittelsen's The Black Death. She journeys a winding fjordside path, by cliff and rock; a black, hooded cloak hiding all but those wide eyes, cold and grey. In one hand she carries an upright rake that some may escape, but her broom will catch all.

Kittelsen is born in southern Norway, 1857; 11 years old when his father dies, leaving him to work as an errand-boy. His artistic gift recognised at 17, he studies in Oslo and later Munich, helped by a generous benefactor. That support ends in 1879, Kittelsen leaving to eke out a living as a draughtsman for German magazines and newspapers. In 1882 he's granted a Paris scholarship, but seems lost and longing for the simple life. "It is becoming clearer, and clearer to me what I have to do," he writes, "and I have had more ideas – but I must, I must get home." He returns to Norway in 1887.

The following 2-years find Kittelsen here in Lofoten, with his sister and brother-in-law south of here at Skomvaer Lighthouse. He discovers nature, his greatest comfort, adding text to his emotive collection of drawings.

Our ferry rolls as we pass the coastal ghost town of Hell somewhere outside, Autumnal clouds heavy with rain, billowing seas grey, buckets of white crash against a ferry window barely a metre from my girlfriend's shoulder. The bow rises and drops. There is a shuddering thump, and I worry how the cars below will cope, consoling myself with the Norwegians being old hands with perilous seas.

We push on towards the smaller island of Vaeroy, surely a concoction of a Norwegian Dr Moreau. Gigantic, jagged peaks sprout from smudged ocean gloom, their sides almost vertical, piercing clouds, melded leaden sky. From Sorland wharf, we drive north to a group of buildings dwarfed by the towering 450m Nordlandsnupen backdrop; this place the original hub of Vaeroy, the one-time Lutheran vicarage, now a glorious guesthouse.

"Kittelsen?" Hege asks with raised eyebrows. "*Ja*, but of course. He was here!" She points to the building opposite our own refurbished-chicken-house lodgings, and hunts down a bulky volume from cluttered shelves of books and an odd mix of island birds; some taxidermist's discarded pride and joy. Hege returns with the blue bound, gold-embossed gem, Fra Lofoten, Kittelsen's signature bold and sweeping. "A confident man?" asks Hege, "I am not so sure." She nods her head and again raises her eyebrows. "He was an artist, after all."

That night the wind howls and rattles windows: the same wind Kittelsen knew when sketching and writing here, confiding in the Lutheran priest and compiling Fra Lofoten; leading the acclaimed Norwegian artist Christian Krohg to surmise, "Lofoten is what suddenly has made Kittelsen into the poet and great artist that he is...his vision is universal, unpretentious and explicit." In the morning I linger outside Kittelsen's room next door to ours, soaking up Arctic sun in the lee of those charcoal-shadowed cliffs. Vaeroy crows whirr, and croaks rise from secret stone ledges; others catching cold updrafts to disappear from view.

The next day we're on the island of Rostlandlet – 'Rost' to locals – the pitter-patter of soft rain on an open awning window. At breakfast the morning outside is grey and as flat as Rost, 'flat as a pancake' on tourist brochures, with 640 human inhabitants surrounded by 300-islets and 2.5-million nesting birds on season.

Finn has lived here all his life, takes tourists out to the bird islands, in what was once the island doctor's boat. He peers up at a featureless sky. "Mmmm... maybe not today," he says as he sniffs the air, "it will be better." Intended to put our minds at ease, Finn tells the story of the local church destroyed in an 1835 hurricane; the spire and attached bells blown clear off and dumped on the ground. He'll take us tomorrow, weather permitting, to Kittelsen's Skomvaer.

In the morning we pass the triple-peaked Trenyken, Finn pondering Kittelsen's trolls; and an Italian archaeologist finding a cave with 3000-year-old cave paintings: mysterious red-ochre figures, giant trolls with odd-shaped heads. Finally, there's Skomvaer Island, the last stop till Iceland; not as flat as Rost, the 1887 lighthouse sitting on low green pastures, behind us the sculptured stacks of Kittelsen's bird islands.

Returning to the mainland in 1889, Kittelsen marries; a self-portrait has him bearded, head turned slightly, pale eyes pensive with an intense inner glow that follows me around the room. The brow is slightly furrowed, the hair short and brownish-fair under an artist's deep hessian skullcap; the dark, crumpled, jacket open to reveal a linen shirt and collar.

Life was difficult for Kittelsen, his wife and nine children. As time passed the artist's health failed, the family forced to sell the home and leave for Oslo in 1910. Kittelsen died at age 57, his friend Christian Skredsvig lamenting "There will never be anyone to succeed him. Even the trolls have disappeared for always. At any rate, I have never seen them since."

From the mainland ferry the horizon is blurred, bird islands laden with ethereal swirls. Sheer granite slabs fall to a wine dark sea. Weird rocky knolls are giant trolls, all warts and wild whiskers. Mysterious hunched figures brood in tumbled cloaks, hiding spell books and pondering the ways of timeless oceans. Ragged mountain crags are cyclopean shapes, heads with crooked faces and big noses. Clouded silhouettes are sirens, the wind their toxin song – Kittelsen's visions as mystical as anything Homer imagined.

15

EFFIE AND JIMMY – Chefchaouen, Morocco, 2015

In the morning I wake with the early call to prayer and the howling of dogs that feel inclined to add their voice to proceedings. I drink black coffee and watch each town light fade among rambling blue walls and drifts of valley mist.

Later I head for the edge of town for breakfast, my daily rosewater and honey yoghurt infusion, with dates, fruit and cereal. My walk leads to the town walls where `Jimmy' meets me at the eastern gate. There is the happy clatter of the laundry contingent and the rush of tumbling white water as wet clothes are slapped on smooth rocks, `Jimmy' a black and white cat owned by a local shopkeeper; although I wonder if Jimmy may actually own Farouk.

Today I finally ask Farouk about the cat, and he scratches a whiskered chin. "It is funny that one." He waits to see how interested I really am, and I nod encouragement. "Well, 2-years past, there is a visitor here, a Scotch man. His name is 'Jimmy'.... we have many tourists here." Now, I am definitely curious.

The cat is watching, and Farouk pauses and lowers his voice. "This Scotch man, he stays for many days; helps my sister in the shop. She tells him he smokes too much... like they are married." Farouk laughs. "He likes my sister, and he is cheeky this Scotch man... very funny, and yes, we are sorry to see him go." The cat has not moved, and Farouk continues. "For many months this man is using the Skype to talk to Effie most days."

"One day this baby cat is here, right at my sister's door. The cat is very small and is demanding food. He is wanting to come inside the shop." Farouk looks across at the gurgling stream. "But Effie can no longer contact her Scotch man. There is no phone. He is suddenly nowhere and she is sad. But this cat, he will not leave this place. 'Jimmy' she is calling him."

16

ESCAPING THE BAKING – Kalaw, Myanmar, 2015

With first sun, Burmese workers arrive crammed in crowded tractor trailers, the clatter of the clapped-out engine jarring. The road from exotic templed plains is already baking, us escaping eastwards to the cool of the mountains, among the lines of buses, cars, trucks and vans. Motorbikes and oxcarts dodge patchwork goats and wandering cattle. All vie for a space on these winding roads.

The crews are dropped off here and there, to fix crumbling bends: women in Coolie sampan hats, long dark skirts and checked shirts shovel and haul buckets of gravel. Faces are sweat and dust laden, daubed with ground bark: the ubiquitous Burmese make-up and protection from a fierce sun.

44-gallon drums stand in groups: asphalt for the mending.
The molten, mess bubbling in coal-fired cauldrons, steaming
and stirred by a cross-legged boy on a raised wooden bench.

17

FADING PHANTOMS – Dili, East Timor, 2013

I am sitting in Melbourne, recalling a visit to one of the world's youngest nations – the Republic of East Timor – just 720km northwest of Darwin. My photographs show a damaged city with bullet-marked buildings; a country scarred by a month-long bout of violence murdering 2000, raping hundreds and wrecking most infrastructure. This was the spiteful aftermath of a referendum showing a clear preference of 78.5% East Timorese in favour of independence from Indonesia.

In 2005 my girlfriend and I arrive at Dili's Hotel Turismo; a quaint piece of `Portuguese Timor' that could be equally be at home in the old colonial Portuguese outposts of Africa or India. We are acutely aware of our country's WW2 debt to this tiny country: 40,000-70,000 local civilians dead due to Japanese reprisals against the Timorese for having assisted Australians. Pink oleanders line the driveway, the jaunty hotel sign classic beachside Art Deco.

In the morning we drive south from a damaged Dili, through rambling hamlets, coffee plantations and eucalypt forests. I ponder the more recent trials of the people here: over 100,000 killed since the 1975 departure of the Portuguese and the occupation by Indonesia (from a population of only 800,000); the killing of 250 demonstrating youngsters at a Dili cemetery in 1991. Only after international pressure did Indonesia agree to the withdrawal of regular troops and the placement of a multinational stabilization force; East Timor independence finally achieved on May 20, 2002

The rugged 4-hour, 70km drive gets us to Maubisse and an old hilltop fort where lawns and gardens swelter in midday heat. From the cool shade of arched Portuguese verandas, we stand and gaze past struggling banana palms that sway in a hot wind, and across surrounding hills that roll and simmer.

At the village of Hato Builico we breathe in the cool evening air, our aim to climb Timor's Mt Ramelau the next morning; the 2962m peak the highest in the old Portuguese empire, and home to the spirits of Timorese ancestors. At 3am our guide wakes us; the narrow beam of his torch cutting through the darkness and entering the door-less opening of our room. We dress in the dark, grab handfuls of muesli bars and gulp muddy mouthfuls of Timorese coffee. It's the dry season and our guide has blankets; we're warned the summit can freeze.

José is 18 years old, with a firm handshake and perfect English. He talks glowingly of a plumber from Sydney, "a good man who came here to teach." José has "many relatives" in Darwin. I see his frown in the light of my girlfriend's torch. He worries about the future, the return of the "old men" who insist on Portuguese as the European language of choice alongside the indigenous tongue of Tetum. "What good is such a thing?" He pleads. "It is the will of these men, who have returned from exile far away; maybe Portugal or Mozambique. 40% of our population are under 15 years old. And I too am young, speaking only Indonesian, Tetum, and English."

Heading across the road to pick up the mountain track, we clap gloved hands together to warm them, and wrap scarves even tighter. We must rush to catch the sunrise. "Hurry, hurry," we're urged, José's tone insistent. We pass the cemetery, the bulk of Catholic graves merging with darker shadows in the inky gloom. We trudge forever upwards as fast we can; our torch beams criss-crossing searchlights, the echo of our boots on gravel louder than expected.

It has been 2-hours and José waves us on. But I am slowing down, listening to my laboured steamy breath as the cold pre-dawn light discloses surrounding hills of desolate rubble and half-built circular huts; wattle-daub walls and bare stick rafters reminiscent of American Indian tepees. At the top, another 3-hours, we are suddenly exposed to the elements. José passes out the blankets and I hunch over in the thin icy air to catch my breath. We huddle under the 3m statue of the Virgin Mary, the wind tearing at blankets beanies and scarves. My feet are cold and my nose runs like a tap.

Peering eastward, we shelter from the wind in front of Mary and wait for the glow of an early sun; the clouds streaky and low. With first light I step out to the side and turn, the gale grabbing at my blanket once more, my eyes half closed and watery. It's a bitter wind that comes from the darkness directly to the west, from the Balibo ruins of a hilltop fort and 'Australian Flag House' where journalist Greg Shackleton painted the national flag on a wall in the hope of identifying his group as Australian and non-combatants, as Indonesian special forces overran the fort in 1975. All five young journalists were killed, with a subsequent US-Australian cover-up to protect a tenuous alliance.

At Hotel Turismo next morning we linger out front, gazing across to our next destination; Atauro Island. From the hotel we walk the length of the beach, amble to the ferry and chat with a group of lawyers escaping to the island for the weekend. They point to the wharf and whisper among themselves. Later they talk of Roger East; the Australian journalist investigating the Balibo killings while living at Hotel Turismo in 1975; him in turn dragged through the streets to the wharf, his hands bound with wire, kicked and prodded with bayonets; his body somewhere among the many others washed up on Dili beach.

Today I browse the web in search of the Hotel Turismo. But all I find is a photograph of a boarded-up, desolate looking street frontage, the giant display on a hoarding heralding the progress of the new East Timor: the demolition of the much-loved 1967 Hotel Turismo and its replacement with a modern nine storey apartment block.

I recall our last evening at Hotel Turismo: looking out

from those quaint Portuguese arches while lounging in aging wicker chairs. I remember drinking beer and Trincadiera while shadows wander the `Casablanca' beer garden; the phantoms of diplomats, revolutionaries, reporters and spies. A tropical breeze carries the past clinks of beer bottles and the excited whispers of young Australian TV journalists in their 20s. I recall rubbing my hand on the rough walls; the very corridors and rooms that witnessed the filing of reports on the Balibo murders of these five young men.

18

FINDING RAJ – Varanasi, India, 2016

I am told Raj is the man. He'll know who I'm looking for, but I find him fast asleep and snoring, call out and wait for him to stir. The *ghats* smell of mould and cow dung, the sticky air grabbing at my drenched shirt and throat. There's the sound of chatter as laundry women slap wet clothes on the steps and water. Raj smiles and wobbles his head from one side to the other, his lone tooth a beacon in a thin-lipped mouth. "Ahhh", he says, raising his rakish frame onto his elbows, then squinting and peering into a washed blue sky, the blazing sun circled with haze.

"But of course Sir, we have many artists, writers too. Afterall, this is India Sir." His eyes gleam. "And Sir... I am most happy to be helping as one pilgrim to another. Mmmm, are you having any change Sir?" There is a sly sideways glance as

I fumble in my pants for some notes and in one deft movement Raj is suddenly very alive, squatting and peering into the distance. He pockets the notes, adjusts a turban of lopsided rag and then points a bony finger. "See there Sir, this the artist you seek."

I stare, but only see the ubiquitous clatter of ghat-side India. "No, you must be seriously looking Sir. Are you not seeing the white many-storeyed building? The building on the ghats, just above the smaller building with the blue plastic?" I see it now and nod. "Ah yes Sir... she is a very famous artist of course. But Sir, the building, she has many gates. You must be using the backside entrance."

19

THE FLOWER GIRL AND THE LIZARD KING – Paris, France, 2015

There is a raspy laugh, parted purple lips, a toothy gap and shining silver orb perched on a pierced tongue. "French? Me?" Mascaraed eyes shine from an impossibly pallid face. "Like... God no." There's a slight lisp, the word 'God' stretched for effect, the intonation classic Celtic. Layla is barely 120cm tall in patent platform boots shining black; tight, thigh-high and laced. The red pleated skirt is short, holey fishnets with coin-size patches of powder-white skin. She stares straight ahead, dyed raven bob, "badly needing a cut"; head tilted to one side.

I wonder what she is doing here among the buckets, pots and vases of a Parisian cemetery flower stall. "Oh well, it's a promise I guess; like... I made it to myself. And my step-father, he helped." There's a pregnant pause. "Oh... and there was a boy." For a moment those green eyes turn to meet mine, before returning to straight ahead. Her stepfather is a muso, and it's Layla's 19th birthday tomorrow; 'tomorrow' being December 8. I offer to pay for the hydrangea Layla now holds, but she shakes her head.

A stooped matron marches past, blue-rinse hair; a prancing, sculptured poodle on taught diamintie lead. There's a disdained "Hmpff!", and a sideways look to sink a ship. Layla shakes her head, having seen it all before; a lone Goth from a small Irish town near Belfast, now "in the City of Lights till things settle". Layla stares down at the flower in her hand. "The most important kind of freedom is to be what you really are." She pauses to gauge my reaction. Yes, I am familiar with Jim Morrison's prose; Layla surprised, but pleased. "Well, I just know all his stuff. It's... like... you know, he's always around."

To get here I have wandered from Ile de St Louis, by Notre Dame and across a bridge full of padlock dedications from teenage lovers, passing City Hall skaters and the tell-tale swish of steel on ice; a side alley lined with parked bikes ends in a plaza and giant painted face staring from walls of red brick and mortar.

I've headed east to Blvd Voltaire and along Rue de la Roquette: to this rolling tree-lined Bohemian cemetery opened to ease the issues of a rat-ridden city: the 44Ha Pere Lachaise, initially shunned by Parisians until a city Prefect moves the bones of renowned French citizens Moliere and Jean de la Fontaine to here; Moliere the actor at first buried among the unbaptised babies. Chic French urbanites soon follow suit; with aspirations to one day dally with the rich, the famous, the artistic and risqué. There's most of Chopin, his heart in his homeland; the first French President too, having died in bed with his mistress while in the throes of oral sex; and a once-infamous journalist, his reclining and suited form with a prominent sculptured fold in his pants, the bronze bulge polished from the constant rubbing of women wishing to fall pregnant. I am in Paris after all.

I am moved by the tale of Abelard, the great French philosopher: a doomed love affair and an illegitimate child, the man castrated and his lover sent to a nunnery. I stand in silence, their bodies finally together beneath this delicate sepulchre, a pile of lovers' letters just inside the picket fence. Oscar Wilde is here too, convicted of 'gross indecency' in England; now entombed in a lipstick-stained tomb of Egyptian Art Deco once adorned by a well-endowed angel with dangling genitalia.

Layla has seriously black eyebrows plucked within an inch of their life, and permanently raised in questioning mode. She's "into street art and architecture." I see myself at her age: no teetotal Vegan, but maybe just a dash of Goth; me coming out mostly at night, haunting darkened, boozy pubs and doped-up music dives in the company of kindred spirits, 'Morrison Hotel' on constant replay. This girl lets down her guard for a moment, allowing me to buy her peppermint tea and crepes; for me it's a coffee and a shot of brandy. I just can't reconcile the fact that 'The Lizard King' had already been dead for over 20-years when this clean-living, slip of a Goth was born. There is a shrug of black-leather-clad shoulders. She does not see my point and looks down at her watch. Time is short. Layla has an appointment for a haircut, tomorrow the big day.

I wish her a happy birthday for tomorrow. We say our goodbyes, the diminutive 19 year old with a dismissive wave, a raspy laugh and another Morrison quote: "Some of the worst mistakes in my life were haircuts."

Back from the cemetery, it's late afternoon. I peer through frosted attic windows, rubbing the glass to reveal a web of bare winter boughs outside. The iPod strains of The Doors "This is the End" mix with the shouts of French School-kids from the courtyard next door, my cosy apartment a haven to random nostalgic recollections. I wonder what a 19 year old teetotal Goth could possibly have in common with a 69 year old, and recall Layla's knowing smirk at the mention of the singer's age if he were here today. "Well, Jim was in a band called The Ravens you know… before The Doors, and I'm thinking he was just so beautiful: dark clothes and slick leather, those steamy eyes, the shaggy hair, and those sexy cheekbones."

I remember Layla's fading smile, and flashing green eyes shining from smudged pools of black. "Jim… like… he was a true Goth!"

Morrison died in 1971 age 27, either in his bed or bath, depending on who we believe; after leaving the high life of Rock and Roll to live here in Paris for only six months. At first buried in an unmarked grave; then with a simple marker, and then a bust. Both were stolen. With the 2008 hiring of a guard, the pilfering stopped. Now there's a simple block engraved in Greek: 'According to his daimon.'

I am thinking of the legions at Pere Lachaise Cemetery tomorrow, well before dawn: the worshippers, the ageing fans, the lost and musically inclined; and a diminutive but feisty Irish Goth who shares Jim Morrison's birthday; her with a talent for quoting The Lizard King and no doubt holding her own in crowded ques while clasping a single turquoise hydrangea between black finger-less gloves.

20

FROM THE MOUTHS OF SAINTS – Normandy, France, 2016

I peer out from under an arch of stone, this ancient Valery gate; northwards over the Normandy harbour of Somme, my thoughts with a simple French peasant girl and a war that lasts one hundred years.

I imagine the year 1430, Joan bought this way from Crotoy to the north, on her way south to a court and trial in Rouen. The evening is gloomy, the arch wet with sea mist, the watching crowd hushed. They say she is a simple girl, just 13 years old when first bothered by the voices of Saints Catherine, Margaret and Michael: The Archangel Michael head of the heavenly militia and responsible for the balancing of souls on judgment day. It is St Michael and this young peasant girl, who can halt the English, their Protestant heresy and their claims to the French throne.

Two days later I wake to wheeling, screaming seabirds 300km away, chimneystacks and steep slate gables: The Medieval village of Mont St Michel perched on the edge of this mighty rock. The 10th century abbey is high above, like Joan, a symbol of French nationhood. From impregnable city gates I stare, a sweeping 2km causeway afloat these endless mudflats and the ruination of would-be conquerors. This in-domitable rock resisted the English to become a prison after The Revolution and through to 1863; from 1979 a World Heritage site, just now bereft of tourists.

Morning's breakfast is potato and cheese, Calvados with my coffee. I climb cobbled paths that vanish round corners, follow steps and crooked winding ways by steep rooftop slates. Gloom hangs in this thick salty air, a blurred grey sky on a blurred horizon. I lean back on slippery wet cobbles, the gilded bronze form of Saint Michael high atop a mighty spire, sword in one raised hand and a set of scales in the other.

My path rises from the city gate and lower city walls, past nook and cranny, crooked crag and cobbles, crossing the guard room and mighty staircase, through a great studded gate and across suspended passage. Prayers echo, shuffling steps of abbots long gone. On the Western Terrace I gaze across the bay to Brittany, the floating Iles Chausey a source of the cold granite under my feet. I take a deep breath, the cold salt-laden air rich and thick, this mighty edifice safe and sound from a world gone mad. I wonder at the horror of the monks when they get the news, their own patron saint Joan's too: the all-powerful Saint Michael strong enough to save this place from the ravages of a 100 Year War, but not the life of a teenage girl – Joan burned at the stake for the immodesty of wearing men's' clothing and the temerity to suggest that Saints speak in French rather than English.

21

GAUDI ON SUNDAY
– Barcelona, Spain, 2015

In the crowded hotel lobby, my daypack zipper sounds conspicuously loud. I poke a hand inside: a woollen vest, an apple and a light rain jacket – nothing more. I rummage about. Still nothing. Everyone looks when I tip the contents out. A single euro coin rolls across the tiled floor, hits the dark timber architrave with a clunk, bounces off, reverberates and finally settles.

My travel wallet is missing and I feel the silent stare of hotel guests and staff. My passport, tickets, driving licence, US cash and euros. All gone. The receptionist rolls her eyes. "We are so sorry, sir," she says, with an uncomfortable shrug of the shoulders, "but it is Sunday." Apparently, Sunday is not a good day to arrive in Barcelona.

Upstairs in my room, I sit glumly. In the beginning things went according to plan. I arrived by train early afternoon, and easily managed the metro through to Central Station, booking ongoing seats to Cordoba. I even impressed a ticket seller with my vestigial command of Spanish. Using my passport to reserve a seat, I'd returned it to my pack, uncharacteristically after 4-months of travel, on top along with my seat reservation. After all, it was only three more stations and a short 100m walk to the hotel.

But here I am, on my first night in Barcelona, dispirited and flat. I open the shutters to the noises from an alley below and sit on a bench by the window. There is a narrow strip of pale dusk sky, a jagged Gothic facade. In the alley, shadows lengthen and join. A dark-haired woman in an olive duffle coat, black tights and boots stands by the shop walls opposite. She suddenly crouches. With a flourish, there's a thick wave-like white line on the pavement, roughly parallel to the walls. She shuffles, stops and stands, then steps back for a moment to admire her handiwork. The chalk wave follows her down the hill. Now there are people with cardboard boxes. They move to and fro, more and more, till the alley is cluttered. Tourists and locals watch, while the open boxes multiply alongside shops and cafes.

I stare as the boxes' contents are removed and delicately placed on the pavement; a single lit match solving the mystery when a wick ignites in the shadows. Before long there's a rolling sea of tea candles. Students dart this way and that, fine-tuning some grand plan, deftly adjusting the flickering lights. Others follow, relighting any that have spluttered out and died; the boxes taken away by an army of willing workers.

Spirits lifted, I leave my room and escape downstairs. Waves of golden candles shine on wet cobblestones and spill over into the city centre. Strangers in scarves and jackets strike up conversations. A teary kid in a red dress with thick blue stripes can't bear to see even one candle die. She carries a lighter and dashes willy-nilly from one to another, rescuing those flames extinguished by damp air laced with the smells of coffee and seafood. I saunter on, away from the realm of candles until the street lamps' blue glow reflects on a silver moonshine road. Trees with pencil trunks stretch bare fingers skywards between fairy-light threads among twisted facades of Catalan whimsy. Here, eccentricity is the spark of genius.

First thing Monday morning I breakfast on *pa amb tomàquet*, the local toasted bread with garlic, tomato, a drizzle of olive oil and a pinch of salt. At the Australian consulate a stocky, pleasant but sad woman purses her lips as she takes notes. "Ah yes, of course, *Senor*".

"And your passport too?" She raises her eyebrows. "Yesterday?" She nods knowingly. I take a deep breath, resigned to the fact that I'll travel the wilds of Spain with a passport photocopy, and collect a new one in Madrid prior to an Amsterdam flight a month from now.

At the Barcelona police station, I fill out pink forms. A short Cypriot lady in black, excitedly waves her arms, exploding into staccato Greek sentences. The young Spaniard at the desk is exasperated. He's not a policeman but employed by the city to assist with the residue of weekend mishaps. A solemn officer stands either side. It seems the poor woman was knocked to the ground yesterday, when her handbag was snatched when leaving church. Her husband steadies her bruised elbow and says nothing.

"Do speak English, please," the young man pleads for the third time. But she soon slips back into her native tongue. He speaks Catalan and Spanish Castilian, as well as German, Italian, English and a little Swedish…. but alas, no Greek. A Dutch couple cannot stay to fill out forms. Their plane leaves in two hours. With a taxi waiting outside their hotel, their entire luggage having disappeared. A teary American student has lost her purse and credit cards. She had hoped to meet her boyfriend in Paris today.

I am at the police station for almost 2-hours, with a new arrival and a new `Sunday' story every ten minutes. I tell myself that life goes on. There are museums to see, a plethora of wonderful Spanish food and wine. There are ruby-red jugs of sangria, and flamenco senoritas with wild manes of hair, flashing feet and dark eyes that sparkle.

The following Sunday I pause at the corner of Carrer Bailen and Corts Catalanes, where I'm transported to 1926, when a man has fallen on hard times: a broken-hearted, bearded vagrant sworn to life-long celibacy, knocked by a hurtling tram that continued on its way. The man was Antonio Gaudí, the great Catalan architect; for me the life and soul of this place. He was on his daily walk to the site of the dream that consumed his later life: the soaring towers of the Sagrada Familia, the 'cathedral of the poor'.

I see him laying bleeding in the gutter, the gathered crowd not knowing the man dressed in a shabby dark suit with frayed sleeves. Taxi drivers refuse to take him to hospital, fearing they won't be paid. The next day Gaudí's friends find him in a poorer hospital. They beg him to allow them to move him to a better place. But Gaudí refuses, saying, "I belong here among the poor." 5-days later Antonio Gaudí is dead at age 74, his most audacious project mothballed and left in limbo, hanging from the sky as if awaiting his return. There's no money, and no one with Gaudí's visionary zeal, his plans are burned in the 1938 Spanish Civil War.

Now, with Gaudi's dream resurrected, I take the lift, then climb to stony medieval towers Gaudí will never see. I stare at stone clusters of giant red, yellow and orange seed pods, green leaves and white doves about to take flight. Agbar Tower's foreign-looking glass edifice gleams in the distance, alongside the apartments and offices of a modern Barcelona; Gaudi's body in a crypt somewhere far below.

I leave the city via the closest metro, holding my pack in one hand and dragging a small wheelie bag behind. A wizened old woman approaches, waving her finger from side to side, no doubt telling me to secure the strap over my shoulder for safekeeping. Across the street another woman screams. I freeze. One man shouts to another and rushing feet clatter on cobblestones. The distraught woman throws herself in front of a car and yells something in Spanish. The car screeches to a stop. Two young men tear past, the leader clutching a small bag and disappearing down a twisted alley. The unlucky woman has withdrawn cash from an ATM, only to have her bag wrenched from her grip; one young guy distracting her, while another surprises her from behind. And yes, it is Sunday.

22

GHOST TRAILS – Machu Picchu, Peru, 2015

I drop my pack at The Sun Gate, descend the trail to the mud and the fog, Machu Picchu nowhere to be seen. I close my eyes and hear the jingling of bells, the rhythmic tramping of sandaled feet, relays of caravans from far-off jungles and deserts. Shaggy lines of llamas are closer now, breaking into a nervous trot, coloured ribbons waving in thin, cold air. They sense I am here, eyes big and round, pools of black. Flickering eyelashes are white, long and unreal. They turn their heads, and stop briefly. I'm frozen in time – maybe 1460 – llamas pushing past, long necks skinny, craning to see the way ahead. They carry gifts.

Bells are louder as the animals shake their heads, ears

twitching this way and that, complaining of heavy bundles strapped on woolly swaybacks. They stamp feet and spit at their handlers: wild-looking men with pierced noses and harsh voices. Behind are fancy-clad emissaries, walking tall with straight backs; important men in long alpaca cloaks that brush my legs as their owners lift hems clear of the mud at the edges. Courtiers and attendants are next, dressed in blue and saffron macaw feathers, condor-head staffs denote positions of power. The earth thumps with each stride as staff hits stony ground. They pass and I wait, not daring to move, the procession not yet complete. There is shuffling and the clap of hands, a man carried by porters on a raft above their shoulders. The man is unperturbed, head held high, the back of his head above the bobbing mass of toiling attendants, his shining black hair in braids, gold rings that dangle from extended earlobes.

He gazes about, then up to the sky; a royal badge framed with gold, pinned to vicuna vest and cloak, the fabric lined with emerald and turquoise. A coloured headband has feathers of the rare golden hummingbird, but his face is a blur: the face of a king, an untouchable god. I hear the porters' grunts in sparse mountain air, the jostle and push as they guide their load away from the edge of the path. I turn as they pass, dark eyes downcast as they focus on the earth: the stone steps and the splash of mud.

I open my eyes and return for my pack, the spell broken by chatting sisters from Saskatchewan; the fog lifting to reveal terrace after terrace, the famous ruins still somewhere below.

23

GHOSTS IN MURK AND MIST – Venice, Italy, 2010

Broken walls topple, taking their last defenders with them. Canal bridges, city gates and the cathedral burn. Steel clashes with steel, horses' hoofs pound stone roads and women drag screaming children, the old and infirm towards the hills and mountains. Columns groan and collapse in an apocalypse of billowing dust and smoke. But some are lucky, floating silently away in the darkness down the Grand Canal into the harbour. Hauling their boats on to the mud of the nearest islands, they hide among the marshes of the Venetian lagoon.

The year is AD452 and a ruthless Hungarian king has arrived at the bustling port of Altinum. Attila the Hun does a thorough job and departs, only to die a year later on his wedding night. In 1500-years, the rising water and lagoon mud swallow the ruins until stones and masonry are discovered under farmland. I am standing near Marco Polo airport, 12km north of Venice, with my girlfriend. It is April last year, at the site of Altinum city, a little bigger than Pompeii, now rolling fields of soybeans and corn. We are following in the steps of John Ruskin – English writer, philosopher, art theorist and a fine draughtsman – to another city of ghosts, Torcello, named after one of the burned towers of Altinum.

We change ferries at Murano and finally spy the belltower, then some pines and scattered buildings, in Ruskin's words, "like a little company of ships becalmed on a faraway sea". Hedges of honeysuckle and briar are unchanged in more than a century since Ruskin's day. Locanda Cipriani, our cream two-storey doll's-house hotel, over a canal bridge, has stairs up to our quaint room. A balcony overlooks the bridge and the floorboards squeak. The six guestrooms have hosted the likes of Nancy Mitford and Ernest Hemingway. Ruskin, born in 1819, had two great loves: his second wife, Rose, who died at 27 years old, and the Venetian lagoon.

Shadows lengthen. We bask in the early spring sun and the bubbles from a bottle of Veneto prosecco. Drifting across the lawns, jonquils, tulips and espaliered vines is the hypnotic click of garden shears. "You will be taking dinner, sir?" Our waiter stands at attention, cloth over arm. He is wide-eyed. "It is just, sir, that the chef, he leaves after dinner. Everyone leaves the island to return in the morning. It is the way here." Although surprised, I answer that 8pm would be fine.

We are both tired after a romantic late lunch. Upstairs, our dreams are fractured and I stumble across piles of discarded clothes in the dark to realise the offending noise is a telephone ringing. We've slept for 5-hours and it's 9pm.

Downstairs, in a forest of white linen, our waiter seems to smile knowingly, resplendent in white jacket and black bow tie.

After dinner, a blanket of milky constellations stretches across the moonless sky outside. In the shadowy piazza, a cat lazing on a stone chair stretches to its full height. Legend says this carved rock is Attila's throne and anyone who sits here will be married within the year. How it got to this island of mud is anyone's guess. Fuzzy yellow lamps on tall posts guide us to the pier, past a jumble of artichoke paddocks.

At the deserted ferry hut, we are mesmerised by shimmering silver reflections and lapping water that drifts between rows of wooden navigation posts tottering like drunken sentries. Ruskin's Venetian tower lights flicker eight kilometres to the south, mingling with floating stars. I smell brackish water, cut grass and an inkling of my girlfriend's perfume.

Next day at Attila's throne it is difficult to believe this once-city held 20,000 souls. By the 12th century, the canals fill with silt, the water stagnates and malaria is rife. A portico connects the larger cathedral of Santa Maria dell'Assunta with a belltower shrouded in scaffolded renovation cladding the Baptistery, and the oldest church in the Venetian lagoon, the octagonal Santa Fosca.

Crumbling, ragged bricks leave orange dust on my fingers. The ethereal light of Santa Maria dell'Assunta shows the finest serrated acanthus carved into the white marble capitals on the taller colonnades. Ruskin thought them "the best I have ever seen, as examples of perfectly calculated effect from every touch of the chisel". A startling Byzantine mosaic of the Last Judgment warns us to contemplate the future but address our actions now.

We save the redbrick belltower until last, clambering to a height of 60m. It's doubtful Ruskin had any renovations to deal with. But between inconveniently placed scaffolding is the same wild sea wasteland of lurid ashen grey that greeted him, and north, the same purple snow-capped mountains. I imagine new arrivals gazing northward with every snowy sunset, heartbroken, remembering the flames devouring their homes.

Back at the ferry hut I step on the gangplank, turn and take one last, late-afternoon look. The belltower appears desolate, caged in scaffold. A lone seagull wheels overhead in the grey air. The bow washes in time with my breathing. My tattered copy of Ruskin's The Stones of Venice opens at page 19: "The glacier torrent and the lava stream: they met and contended over the wreck of the Roman empire; and the very centre of the struggle, the point of pause for both, the dead water of the opposite eddies, charged with embayed fragments of the Roman wreck, is VENICE."

Disembarking at St Marks, we push past the African bag-sellers, the pickpockets and tour groups. At our heavy cast-iron gate I look back over my girlfriend's shoulder to the far colonnades of the piazza. There, under the portico arches, I imagine Ruskin. He looks frail, not imposing at all, with a tatty grey beard, buttoned vest and oversized coat, his move-ments disconnected and urgent, a wild look in his eye as he bickers and haggles with himself.

After 11-visits, Ruskin knew every corner of this city and

considered himself an adopted son. He first suffered mental illness in 1886, completing his autobiography and the fig-tree sketch in the same year, before following his wife into the abyss of insanity and dying of influenza in 1900.

Turning, I push open the squeaky gate into our deserted hotel courtyard. In the musty air, I run my hand over the cold dome of yet another ancient wellhead. The sounds of St Marks have evaporated and a lamp beckons beneath a white awning.

Early next morning we drink strong black coffee on our balcony above the Orseolo canal. Gondoliers call, mist hangs above the water and we smell freshly baked pastries. A man in a leather apron and floppy tweed cap lugs groceries from a barge below, while a black Labrador sits up front.

Both draughtsmen, we admire a sketch of Ruskin's: The Fig-tree Angle of the Ducal Palace from 1869, all light and shade, eastern arches and colonnades. So... Venice is both East and West, but she is only the daughter, and it all began with another place just north of here: "Mother and daughter, you behold them both in their widowhood, TORCELLO and VENICE."

24

GOLDEN ORBS – Inle Lake, Myanmar, 2015

From a rickety plank jetty, we float south on a Burmese longtail boat, the sun an orange-red disc in an early morning sky of dust and woodsmoke. It is half an hour to Inle Lake: 22 x 10km and only 1.5m deep I'm told, mingling at the edge with an overgrown riot of green, and no telling where the real lake starts and finishes.

Our helmsman-guide balances bolt upright, toes grip the flimsy hull. He peers ahead from his perch on the very end and lifts the long shaft clear to pull lotus roots from a strangled prop. Another hour and we push into the maze of channels proper, sliding past raised thatch or rusted roofs, and eventually see the golden top spire of our goal – the 100m high Phaung Daw Oo golden pagoda.

The boat is tethered midst a menagerie of others, our

stepping stones from one boat to another; then stairs up to leave sandals on burning stone pavers. There's relief in the dark of shaded stalls and shops; the chatter, the brass Buddha masks and coloured tees, the pungent wafts of incense, the chimes and carvings. More steps and we're inside the great hall, and an all-enveloping silence, the porcelain tiles cool and white. A central pedestal stand is a metre diameter and sits on a locally raised red floor, an ornate gilded canopy hangs from high temple ceilings.

On the stand are five golden single or double orbs, the size of large bowling balls, each distorted and different from the other: what's left of 800-year old Buddha statues, each having collapsed under the weight of gold leaf offerings applied by devoted male pilgrims passing this way.

Each year the Buddha's images are transported by barge, visiting the fourteen lake villages and monastery with great ceremony. In 1964, with the sinking of the barge in rough weather, one of the precious Buddhas is lost overboard. Miraculously though – with all hope gone – the deformed statue is found waiting on its pagoda pedestal to be reunited with its four companions upon the barge's return.

25

HAPPY NEW YEAR FRANK – New York, USA, 2014

A guy has fallen on hard times, huddled under gentrified tenement stairs; on one side his clapped-out shopping trolley bound by trash bins and black cast iron pickets. The stairs span from street side pavement up to an ornate doorway, moulded guardian face glowering overhead. He seems in his 60s, but his real years are anyone's guess. One day I ask, but my question is met with a non-committal nod of his grey face and averted blue eyes. The voice is a low cigarette-drenched rumble, sentences broken with a retching hack of a cough.

"Yeah, times are not so good buddy; rents are steep." There is a raspy sigh of resignation. "It's still home though." He peers up and down the street and waves a bony hand. "I know every alley, and every dry spot in this town." This time the cough seems a little self-conscious. "I moves around a bit."

His name is Frank. "Like the singer," he croaks. "You know, as in Sinatra." I'm thinking more Tom Waits in a ratty leather cap with ear flaps. We have been here for two weeks now; our plan being for a white Christmas and New Year in the comfort of a designer apartment. Passing Frank most nights, we sometimes offer food leftovers, always accepted – remnants of New York dinner serves far too big – pizza, Hungarian meatballs, the occasional doughnut or giant cinnamon pretzel.

It's New Year's Eve and we grip throwaway cardboard cones in gloved hands, munching on the sweetest red strawberries pre-dunked in dark chocolate, ambling on 5th Avenue en-route to Times Square. We have an early evening play booked, followed by finger food and drinks in a `Warming Lounge'; all planned 6-months previously, pre-empting our anticipated entry to the legendary Times Square Ball Drop viewing.

Turning off 2nd Avenue early morning, our steps echo close to home now, the air chilly, street lamps a dull golden glow. Our steamy breaths dissolve in damp night air. My whiskered face is cold, but I am warm in my mandatory hiking boots, woollen cap, Wind stopper jacket, scarf and thermals.

There is the distant bleep and whoop of police cars towards Alphabet City. I pause for a moment. There is a stirring off to one side, a voice from the gloom seemingly insistent, laboured but loud. "Hey buddy!"

I freeze for a moment, with sudden flashes of an East Village that once was; a rough and tumble place of ramshackle squats, risks and rougher times. I am so close to the voice, I smell wet wool and cigarette smoke; but really, there is no need to worry. He is hunkered down in blankets and plastic sheets; Frank's voice deep and worn as always. "Happy New year," he says.

26

KARTHIK AND THE KILLER PARROT – Doha, Qatar, 2014

I remember one night in Doha, chatting with a traveller-friend with the background hum of a busy airport terminal and the smell of coffee from a nearby cafe. We've first met in Lagos and are sitting in a lounge whiling away hours waiting for flights: me to Korea and Karthik to Mumbai. Karthik is wide-eyed and tugging my shirt sleeve. "Your India book, I am reading Sir," the sudden admission a surprise with Karthik not normally so forthcoming. "It is true you walked across my city of Mumbai Sir?" I nod, and there is a self-conscious cough. "You are being a serious writer Sir, and must be doing the needful to write more on such serious adventures."

I'm not sure about the 'serious' bit, as my writing `career' has spawned little recognition or income, but Karthik's plane is finally on the tarmac and he fiddles with a bag of duty free. He's a young guy, about 30 years old, a FIFO commuting between the oil and gas hub of Nigeria and his home.

He gets lonely in Lagos he says, and has now bought a pet parrot, "for the company Sir." I can't help but smile, and there's an indignant grimace. "But Sir, you must be knowing he is very intelligent... an African Grey... the most intelligent of birds Sir."

I wonder at the logic of sharing a small Lagos room with an African parrot called Shiva, when that feathered, beady-eyed beastie can't be trusted: Karthik forced to wear pink wash-up gloves and is savagely bitten while cleaning the bird's cage or offering food.

But that bird really is smart, for even the gentle, kind-hearted and organised Karthik has bad days; sometimes leaving the cage door open, the vicious bird refusing to budge, knowing better than to take on the wilds of downtown Lagos. One thing for sure though: Without this `serious' career of mine, I really would miss the stories... the happy and the sad, the tragic, the ridiculous and funny... like the mystery of why a fresh-faced Indian would share a cramped room with a blood-thirsty parrot.

27

A LONG HAUL –
Mandalay, Myanmar,
2016

Yangon station is dark at 5:30am, faded columns tatty in this clammy colonial gloom. Commuters wander to and fro, bags on the platform of this and that. My `upper seat' ticket costs US$8 for the 600km trip, `life insurance' less than one cent; `upper level' meaning superior class. We're away with a toot, a grind and a shudder. Seats are grotty and torn, paint flaking from a worn-out frame. Bags and hats hang from the occasional hook.

It's a rocking-rolling ride with bouts of kangaroo hops. Outside the light strengthens, woodsmoke drifts in layers, winter sky faded, the clatter and roar broken by occasional toots from the engine. At the approach to each station the crowd noise rises, the mantra of waiting trader hordes that jump onboard and walk the length of the train, acrobat vendors balancing plated offerings on their heads. Windows are all pulled open, some relief against the stifling closeted air.

A crimson-clad monk throws an empty water bottle through an open window. Across the way a doting father holds his only son close, me the star attraction. I stare out the windows, the Burmese countryside floating past; at the white pasted faces of workers, giant white pigs and yellow melons stacked by rickety sheds and lean-tos. A guy in a checked shirt is perched on a tiny motorcycle, 2-women riding side-saddle hang on the back. A girl with a parasol harangues a herd of patchwork goats, a buffalo glistens and sways while hauling a wooden trailer. There are women with sampan hats in backwater lotus ponds by dry rice paddies.

Village locals ply their trade on dusty tracks: water, bananas, yellow cobs of corn, greenish oranges and plastic packets of sunflower seeds up and down the swaying aisle. There are silver platters of tandoori chicken on long sticks, bottles of whisky, warm lemonade and beer. Warbled Burmese music blares from a mobile up the back, dampened by train track clatter and vendors' calls in this crowded carriage – all as if from a crackling gramophone in the midst of a storm.

After 15-hours I'm exhausted as we pull into Mandalay, my throat dry; my little friend still in his father's arms and sharp as ever. He's had a short nap midway, with not a whimper the entire journey.

28

LONGINGS AND LEFTOVERS – Farmington, USA, 2012

We fly from Melbourne to New York, continuing on to Pittsburgh. We're in this part of the country to see the `best example of American architecture', the iconic creation of Frank Lloyd Wright. The hire car attendant is astounded anyone would travel this far, handing over the keys to our 4WD; my girlfriend hoping for snow. We head for our overnight stop at the old Fayette Springs Hotel.

On our arrival we're greeted with a surprise; this place no country diner. Andrew Stewart had high aspirations; a local land baron, an ambitious and driven man with a serious longing to succeed. He set the bar high in everything he did, building this grand retreat in 1822. In the tavern, over mandatory Dirty Martinis, I ask a local if he knows the identity of the resident ghost. He shakes his head. "Nope. Sorry." He looks up and down the bar. "There're stories of course. By the way, which room you got? Ah huh! The one on the right?" He frowns, nods his head slowly up and down and tugs at his cap peak. "Mmmm, yep, that's the one alright."

From a shared dinner of mussels `Black and Blue', with a terracotta bottle of Cherokee wine, we climb winding stairs to our attic room. Timber steps and balustrades creak, crooked floors are covered in thick red carpet. In the darkness small windows rattle and rafters shake with the approach of a northern storm. What dastardly act led to our restless spirit being relegated to some parallel world? I'm thinking some tragic longing, a drowning, a suicide or triple murder; the dull clanking of rusted chains, a tear-stained wretched face with hollow eyes. The door rattles.

In the morning we stand on Stewart's raised porch by palatial carved columns, in the lee of his beloved Laurel Highlands; these columns reminders of the success of Ancient Greece or Rome, and the aspirations of Mr Stewart. I doubt Lloyd Wright would have approved, but from here Stewart surveyed all he owned.

I rub my hands and stamp my feet; my girlfriend wide-eyed at the rolling mountains swathed in white. A rusty pick-up truck passes, with bumper-mounted plough, pushing snow off to one side; another slides through the carpark in a sweeping turn. I tread gingerly across the icy patio, down to a pile of white; our parked car. My boots sink in squeaky powder snow. The engine turns and I slam the door, shovelling snow from the roof and sides; my girlfriend's son scraping ice from the windows. I grab deep cold breaths and exchange glances with my girlfriend. At home it's 37degC, with sun lotion and swimming the order of the day.

Climbing into the Laurel Highlands, I'm thinking of Congressman Stewart, who at his final reckoning must have been intensely disappointed. For after going to the trouble of handing out masses of free watermelons to voters, the wrong name was mistakenly recorded for the position of Vice President of the USA – Stewart being the pre-agreed preference – thereby thwarting any chance he had of becoming President.

29

LOOKING FOR A LIFE – Lagos, Nigeria, 2016

Mosque minarets pierce soggy Lagos skies and I ask my driver to stop, the road potholed with waterlogged lakes and lined both sides with traders' stalls. Just here are piles of tomatoes on tottering stacks of pavers. Ribs sizzle next door, sweet basil wafting from the meaty pile frying over open flames.

Rasheed's seat is a round rusted drum, his skullcap like his teeth, a dazzling white. In the middle of his forehead, the tell-tale callouses from years of prostrating 3-times daily, his head touching the ground God-knows how many times. He looks right through me, his eyes cloudy, white swathed arm outstretched in my direction. "You will buy something Boss," he says, and smiles "… inshallah." The tomatoes hail from somewhere "up north" … like his family. His wares are shining egg-like orbs. They are bright red these tomatoes, meticulously and proudly set in assorted round bowls in seemingly impossible pyramids.

His brother was the first to arrive years ago, convincing his mother to follow with Rasheed, from a family of twelve. His father had died "many years passed". The others stayed and Rasheed shakes his head. "Don't know what happened Boss." He falls silent, shuffling selected tomatoes from one precarious pile across to another.

There's a noise from the road – the rush of rumble of an engine, and a splash – and we both turn. A woman stands straight and tall, balances a wide dish on her head like a black Carmen Miranda. She waves her arms and yells at the top of her voice, the square loaves of bread on her head still. I watch as she turns her head from left to right, steps out and floats across the road through a calf-deep pond, oblivious of any hidden holes, rocks and broken pavement, her feet feeling the way.

From the mosque it's a half hour drive back to my apartment, passing family stalls and lean-too shops selling this and that. A makeshift newspaper stand is laden with papers and the occasional magazine, all spread on a crooked trestle. Headlines hang from bulldog clips on a rope strung between wooden legs: An Imam killed up north, more kidnappings, and thirty students all shot as they slept in their school dormitory.

I peer out my apartment window, over an ancient

generator that rattles more than hums. A roving street butcher has burned off the fur from a once brown goat, the flash of knife and machete with the ritual of cleaning and hacking now begun. Neighbours have left baskets to claim their share and a black pall of smoke rises to meld with these grey-laden skies.

It's another week when I next see Rasheed from a distance, him finished for the day, standing and adjusting his pure white robes. There's a young girl too. They talk and I watch as they leave together, Rasheed with one hand on her shoulder, a stick in his other hand. The girl is of smallish frame, maybe 12 years old, with bright eyes and a pitch-black face that beams out from under her pink hijab. She leads, steps lightly, the pair now moving as one, the girl attentive, looking about them, then up and down.

As we drive past I turn in the seat, the pair negotiating the opposite side of the road, Rasheed's stare fixed straight ahead as they fall again into common stride. Rasheed's stick is held tight, prodding ahead with a splash as it hits the flooded pavement. The girl stops again, another drain across their path. Something is said and they set off once more, pick up the pace and glide as one. With the sinking sun I wonder how long it will be for Rasheed to reach `home'.

30

LOST DOGS – Lofoten, Norway, 2014

"Puffin dogs?" Hege shakes her head. "You know, there are none on the island at this point in time?" I'm speechless with disappointment. "*Ja,*" she adds, "but there were hundreds here last week." It seems we have just missed the Norwegian Lundehund Club 50 Year Anniversary – a meeting of puffin dogs from around the world.

Vaeroy ('Weather Island', population 780) lies off the southern tip of the north-western Norwegian Arctic Archipelago of Lofoten; an 'awe-inspiring' part of the world according to National Geographic. Magical Vaeroy has cave paintings, Northern Lights and soaring birdcliffs inundated with 1.5-million nesting seabirds in summer; eagles, kittiwakes, cormorants, auks, eider petrels... and puffins: the cute yet fierce adult with a powerful neck and beak, along with razor-sharp talons; the single chick so spoilt and fat, that only after days without food can it wriggle from the burrow to be pushed, or 'puffed', by the adults to the sea, before it can fly.

To get here my girlfriend and I have driven 250km south-west from Tromso, off-season late August to avoid excessive tourists and twitchers; the downside being no nesting puffins. We are staying at the northern end of Vaeroy in Hege's `Chicken House', in what was once part of the Lutheran vicarage. In the morning we head for the old airport, a failed enterprise plagued with irregular flights in viciously unpredictable winds. A terrible accident in 1990 left all passengers killed, the captain's body never found. It is an odd feeling gazing over the intact but eerily deserted tarmac as wind whistles around the control tower.

Today's 2-hour hike begins west of the tower, now a chocolate factory and shop. Our path follows the west coast on a high, narrow, muddy track and low scree beaches with rock scrambles over flotsam, jetsam and bleached driftwood. Waves crash over a giant cylindrical buoy, ripped from some distant ocean mooring, its yellow casing cracked open, its flotation innards exposed.

At the low Isthmus of Eidet we cross on the remnants of an all-weather road, a ragged row of rough-hewn flag-stones each side, emerging above the even wilder waters of the eastern shore. We turn south to climb a narrow, exposed path cut from the mountainside; rusted chain between us and the wild surf far below. Around a corner we halt to take in the immensity of the granite-gneiss backdrop against the Lilliputian gaggle of huts propped at its base. This is what's left of Mastad, the birders' town – once home to 150 hardy souls and their puffin dogs – mostly dismantled and reused in the new but distant town centre of Sorland.

Our path leads down to village flats, across moss-laden culverts and tumbledown stone fences adorned with splashes of early-autumn wildflowers. Broken paths and retaining walls testify to the birders' existence. The timber grain of a weathered wall feels proud at my fingertips, the wooden boards coursed by innumerable Arctic winds. I kneel and push groundcover leaves away from sprigs of tiny blueberries; slightly sour, crunchy and delicious. Listening to the surf battering the ancient stone slipway, I search for more berries and inadvertently smear blue dye on my face. The mud by my boot has revealed a prehistoric six-toed paw print, a strange double-jointed dog with extra grip that can turn its head 180-degrees back over its own spine.

Next night we dine in Sorland with Aina and Rob. "Tough? I guess so." Rob shares the Norwegian gift for understatement. The people lived from fishing and birding with the men on the ocean most days. The women and children handled the gathering of puffin chicks to make ends meet.

"You know, Norway in those days was very poor, something difficult for the young to understand.'" Rob paused, looking across at the kids playing. He smiles. "*Ja*, the harbor at Mastad was dangerous, with sunken reefs, the town so isolated. We have hurricanes, and serious whirlpools here;

the history books show us deaths each month." Rob draws a slow breath, recalling the tough conditions. "Once a great storm hoisted a three-tonne stone and threw it, blocking the slipway. Rogue tides ripped at birders' huts, dragging them to the sea."

But what of my Vaeroy puffin dogs? "Ahhh," adds Rob, "they climb rocky places, crawling into holes to bring back the chicks unharmed. In one night a good dog could bring over twenty. They are clever, these dogs; alert and watchful, but wary of strangers." The breed was once only found on that tiny pocket of Mastad beach, and was not destined for an easy life.

Puffin netting began in the 1850s, neglected dogs killing sheep for food. On Rost to the south, government taxes made dog ownership a financial liability until only 50 remained here on Vaeroy; descended from ancient, pure stock that supplied a mainland breeding program in 1939. In 1943 the breed was formally recognized, only to see distemper sweep Vaeroy killing all but one of the island dogs; resulting in two pregnant bitches and two puppies arriving from the mainland to repopulate the island.

A further distemper epidemic swept the mainland the following year, with limited reinforcements this time sent from Vaeroy. By the 1970s, Vaeroy puffin dogs had been exported to other European countries, thereby saving the breed from extinction. In 1987 the first puffin dogs arrived in America, leading to 700-800 now worldwide.

Although marvelling at such a twisted story, I am feeling low. Our preference for travelling off-season has hijacked my plans to meet a Vaeroy puffin dog, and we board the ferry for

Rost. At breakfast the morning is grey and as flat as Rost – `flat as a pancake' in the tourist brochures – with 640 human inhabitants surrounded by 300-islets, and 2.5 million nesting birds in season, including puffins.

When I mention my fruitless quest to the hotel receptionist, there is a quizzical look. "But they have all gone north of course, with the herring." I wonder why the dogs would have gone even further north than Vaeroy. Once outside, my girlfriend looks at me and rolls her eyes, the receptionist obviously bamboozled by my rapid-fire colonial English, believing I was asking about the puffins.

On our early-morning walk, cats stare from beneath crooked cod racks. Dogs bark from behind a dockside house with high-pitched, insistent yaps. Could it be? We exchange glances and I turn towards the source of the sound. 3-dogs strain at their leashes; the size of large cats, fox-like harlequin faces, white with black markings, round brown eyes, sharp-looking teeth, pointed ears, white chests, short tan, black-tipped fur; bushy tails curl upright.

I have finally found my Vaeroy puffin dogs here on Rost, a trifle feistier than expected. In fact, they are definitely not as happy to see me. I courageously step forward; the barking rises several decibels, and in my best Norwegian I attempt to explain how happy I am that they haven't flown north.

31

LOST PEARLS AND POMEGRANATES – Andalusia, Spain, 2015

The phone rings late afternoon: my girlfriend having just arrived. We meet and trudge uphill from Granada station, through the 15th century Gate of Pomegranates to this Alhambra citadel of ruddy stone towers, roses, oranges and myrtles, a garden-fortress built to house a Moorish army of 40,000.

The last Sultan was born here, Boabdil imprisoned in the Tower of Comares when newly married; by a paranoid father who once ordered the beheading of 36-knights in the Hall of the Abencerrajes, the red stains still shouting from fountain bases and flagstone floors. Boabdil escaped from his prison on a rope of his mother's silken scarves.

Castellated battlements throw jagged shadows, the flags of Granada, Spain and Andalusia flapping in a late spring breeze; that of the European Union a reminder of Napoleon's retreating army mining the place before leaving, this World Heritage wonder only saved by a Spaniard cutting the fuse to a French stash of gunpowder.

70km south lay a snow-capped mountain horizon, our destination Las Alpujarras – 80-ish oasis villages straddling streams in Sierra Nevada foothills – higgledy-piggledy, white-washed boxes in jumbles of stark, scoured canyons; groves of almonds, olives, oranges and lemons, terraced pastures and rambling orchards: cherry, chestnut, fig, and flowers wild. Later we stare from lofty Alhambran balconies, the sun sinking low, over brumous canyon depths and the Moorish Albaicin. Cool mountain breezes roam rustic walls, gardens and alleys. Fountains splash below scalloped porticos and shadowed halls.

Boabdil would finally depose his father in 1482, only to be captured the very next year by Castilian Catholic armies; his own son taken hostage as security and Boabdil left as care-taker only. After 6-years of war with his father and uncle, Boabdil was again besieged by Castilian armies, exiled to Las Alpujarras and mostly remembered for leading a small band of dejected followers to a mountain pass and bursting into tears when turning back to gaze on a distant Alhambra for one last time: his lost 'pearl set in emeralds'. Our aim is to follow in the footsteps of Boabdil.

The morning bus leaves Granada, reaching Lanjaron within the hour. Another hour, and we're by the fertile Guadalfeo River and the largest village Orgiva, palisaded by lemon, olive and orange groves; the road finally climbing into the Sierra Nevada. At 1200m, Pampaneira has a busy village square with plastic café chairs, coloured rugs on merchants' racks, gaggles of artisans' stores side by side. Open channels gurgle and rush, water tumbling all the way to the River Poqueira. We buy sausage and bread, red wine and green olives,

Clusters of whitewashed homes cling to rock walls, skirted by twisting cobbled paths; terraces first tended by Moors planting mulberry trees to feed silkworms for busy Almería mills. Snowmelts become freshwater, the Sierra Nevada shelters villagers from the worst of freezing winter winds. Bubion is a mere 100m uphill; a winding gravel path between drifts of poppies: splashes of red that sprout from ancient rock piles, broken bricks and Moorish dreams. We pass orchards, poplars and vegetable plots. A crucifix hangs from a laundry wall, while cobbled paths wind under flower-filled balconies and past a 16th century church built by converted Moors. A ruined fortress sits silent.

Red and white trail markers line a narrow dirt road. We amble beneath chestnuts and holm oaks. Snow-powdered peaks hang from the relentless blue of Spanish skies. On a rubble track I stare north, along the 'Ravine of Blood', to another wave of a distant village: whitewashed blocks perched on a shimmering rocky saddle. We cross the Las Alpujarras road, descending village alleys and twisted way, past fountains and concrete troughs loaded with geranium clusters of lipstick-red. Sheep and goats ramble sloping paddocks;

an ancient olive showing the way, its gnarled trunk striped white and red.

A 10min track falls to the village of Pitres, between stands of walnuts and cherries. Large homes nestle on higher wooded terraces. Chaparrals are scarlet roses, lining cobbled, tinkling channels of cold mountain water, falling to the sister hamlets of Mecina, Mecinella and Fondales; paths through an urban Moorish maze, between odd-angled walls, and finally standing on the Trevelez.

At 1200m, Ferriola emerges from the green of unruly fig thickets. A broken pomegranate tops the gateposts, the symbol of Boabdil's Granada. We amble on tessellated grey slate between two walls, under wooden beams and someone's living room to sip peppermint tea in a shop doorway. A tabby cat sprawls in afternoon sun, among TV aerials, chimney toadstools and straggling rooftop wildflowers.

Past an open trough of a laundry, we find a bar and buy costa in a plastic Coke bottle; a local concoction somewhere between moselle and sherry. Tonight's lodgings are converted stables – our Swedish hosts living above – whitewashed walls and beams, a low rickety door; winding steps down to a cave-like bedroom, bathroom and rustic sunken kitchen. In the morning I pay Sven and wonder what a Swede is doing way down here. He laughs, and answers in perfect English. "Ahhh yes, I see… we are great walkers, and have been many places." He tweaks the end of a white pointed beard. "It is the ghosts that keep us here."

It's 5-minutes to La Gaseosa, a fizzy-sweet mineral-water fountain spouting from a blue and yellow mosaic tiles into a concrete basin. Tied twisted twigs make an artwork of a farm stock gate. At the Busquistar turn, a shale path weaves past dishevelled stone shepherd huts and walls, across dry wild country falling again to the gurgling Trevelez. Ducking under a wooden lintel to enter Moorish ruins; the mill's walls broken and tumbled down. We share plastic cups of the yellow-brown costa.

In the morning we leave a sleepy Notaez on a goat track across rolling hills, the ground damp, pungent thyme and rosemary crushed underfoot. From here it's mostly uphill to Castaras, then Nieles, to a flooded crossing and cold feet: the recently swollen Guadalfeo. We arrive in the dark, wet and bedraggled to the welcoming luxury of Alqueria de Morayma. There is almond soup, pork and lamb; us on wooden stools by crackling log fire and bar. My thoughts settle on Boabdil and his 15 year old bride; the 'tender Morayma'.

In the morning we wake to sun on shining white walls across the valley, and complaining turkeys penned just outside. Our bus leaves the Cadiar square, by a 16th century Renaissance church. Old men in tweed jackets and ties are lost in conversation and clouds of cigarette smoke. At Ugijar, we're almost at the end of our quest and our journey's most eastern reach.

Boabdil was here for less than a year when Isabella, on the advice of her Catholic confessor, banished him from Spain; his people here for another 100-years, until they too were expelled around 1570, leaving two families of Moors per village to teach newcomers farming and water management.

I wipe sweat from my neck with a grotty bandanna, our trail leading upward along a dusty, dirt road; past endless olive rows all the way to Las Chimeneas guest house. Late afternoon we sit drinking Spanish beer and take in the perfumes of a Moroccan tajine. Smoking logs burn in a cast-iron stove; clouds journey overhead, shifting shadows on rolling hills and a distant Mediterranean.

Next morning there is one last thing: to follow a creek through stands of pines, skirting snowdrifts to lunch on Mulhacen's 3600m shining white cap: the burial place of Boabdil's cruel father. Panoramic views stretch north to Granada and south over coastal hills, the Mediterranean, and on to Morocco, the Rif Mountains and the World Heritage city of Fez; where Boabdil `The Unfortunate' fell in 1527, fighting an obscure battle for some obscure African cause.

32

MANDELA DAY – Johannesburg, South Africa, 2015

Back in Johannesburg for an extended African stay, I have been away for over 35-years. This time there is no immigration paperwork and I am simply issued a visa at the airport. From Perth it's been an 11-hour flight, across the Indian Ocean, skirting Mauritius and Mozambique. The city is waking to another sky of azure blue, the signature of a high veldt winter. But there are looming clouds: the uncertain health of the elder statesman Nelson Mandela, a remarkable man having once inspired a young Barack Obama to urge his college board of trustees to divest South African investments as a protest against this country's then apartheid policy. The future US President would eventually meet Mandela in 2005;

the American by then a Democratic senator. One year later, Obama would visit Cape Town and stand silent and sombre inside what was once Mandela's cramped Robben Island cell.

From a construction-riddled airport I pick up a hire car and drive to a crowded supermarket; directed into a parking bay by a skipping black man in a fluoro yellow vest and a jaunty pork pie hat. Afterwards I pack my shopping in the boot and hand my parking assistant a silver two Rand coin, heading back into the traffic fray and towards my walled estate accommodation.

There is a lumbering Metrobus belching smoke from a shaky exhaust pipe that hangs low to the road. There seems less of the soaring ring of tailings dumps that once encircled this vibrant `world class African city'; many of the man-made mountains having been dismantled for what's left of the gold. African trinket-sellers wander between the slow-moving cars and I daydream of another time; me waiting for a 'white' bus, while several `black' buses pass, packed with gleeful dark faces; me having to wait on the corner under their hot African sun.

I recall walking into a red brick building back then – government I think – but with two entrances, with 'my' door to the right and another at the far end; once within, the two queues merging side by side and leading to a single long service desk of gleamingly grand mahogany. The longer row of blacks is separated from the whites by a single partition rope sagging between two tottery poles; the shuffling queues less than 2m apart.

Today my apartment is well-appointed and comfortable,

but life here somehow lacks the exuberance and mischief of Hillbrow, in the Jo'burg centre I once knew; a hybrid of high rise towers and condominiums, where I returned one night to my serviced apartment and was greeted with a cupcake I've left behind, only someone has taken a bite; a calling card of my long-time maid who had cheekily returned it to my kitchen bench. There was help with the car parking in those days too, wanted or not, with much theatre and shouting; maybe even a dance. A cross word to the locals and there was a good chance the hubcaps would be missing on your return.

These days, I'm told it's a dangerous place; an over-crowded no-go metropolis infamous for squatters, guns and New Year's Eves where white goods, beds and TV's are thrown from upper apartments to city streets and pavements below: out with the old and in with the new.

I read of the US singer-songwriter Sixto Rodriguez, his recent visit prompting memories of a 1974 free open-air concert, me surrounded by excited young Jo'burg whites with heads and hearts full of the mythical magic of a Rodriguez then thought dead in a politically isolated and closed-off country; his music circulated on pirate cassettes that encapsulated the hopes and dreams of these kids' younger years. I remember sharing bottles of whisky and news from the outside world, me an oddball bearded longhair from somewhere else, all of us enraptured on the day by another musician: A South African icon; the Manchester born Johnny Clegg, an early master blending Western pop with African Zulu.

It seems a century ago when I last left, with Nelson Mandela then languishing in prison, me flying to Rhodesia, now Zimbabwe, and then on to Angola: a colonial outpost with the Portuguese on the verge of leaving after a bloody fifteen year war; the heat explosive, the air intimidating and oppressive, the stuffy transit lounge sweltering, sweaty, and swathed in cigarette smoke.

It's nightfall outside, and I rub my eyes fearing an impending dose of jetlag. The apartment is silent, my dozing fitful. I wake with clammy hands and visions of Portuguese marines with oversized automatic weapons; gun belts slung over mottled shoulders, jungle battle greens hanging limp on tense statues with eyes hidden by dark aviation sunglasses.

In the morning I wake to more sad news of Nelson Mandela; critically ill in hospital for 5-weeks now. Known here as`Madiba', the name of his tribe, he will be 95 on the 18th July; internationally known as `Mandela Day' since 2010.

Suburban lights flicker in the gloom outside my window. There is the melancholic cry of some African bird, and the first hum of distant highway traffic. The king size bed looks far too big and I have time on my hands to ponder the changes of the last few decades.

But it is not the dangers of being in the wrong place at the wrong time that dominate my foggy thoughts. It is not the cut and thrust of travel, the chance meetings of like-minded souls on similar paths, or the comings and goings of relationships over time. And it is not even the failing health of Nelson Mandela; once imprisoned for 27 years for upholding his principles of human equality. I am thinking of another world when all South Africans were not equal, me sitting in a Johannesburg dentistry all those years ago, peering through a half-closed doorway into a cupboard of a waiting room, where a sullen black man had waited for most of the day;

doubled over, pallid and moaning with pain, until the last white had been attended to; me, with a small chip off the corner of my tooth.

33

MEETING SAINT LOUISE – Trondheim, Norway, 2013

We had passed by here before, tall and ornate, diamond timber-panelling on grand double gates always shut; the name in sweeping letters across the arched pediment above. This time on the way to Nidaros cathedral, I pay little attention, until my girlfriend stops. Today, it seems an inset central door is open. We brave the stream of darting cyclists to cross the cobblestone road. From the open door a sumptuous courtyard unfolds; sunlit, lush but apparently deserted. Another bicycle leans on a rendered wall, the 50-apartment building classic Berlin Baroque. A kneeling woman sculpture bathes by a sprinkling fountain, blue water in pools offset; splashes of pink hydrangea in orotund urns.

A man appears suddenly and looks up – a wiry customer with round-rimmed glasses and a ready smile, spade in hand. "A wonderful garden," I offer. His eyebrows raise and we're unprepared for his rapid reply, even with English is no surprise here. "Thank you," he says, head slightly to one side, "you are Australian?" Geir is a sailor, the water close to all Norwegians' hearts, but having braved the Queensland molasses run of the 1960s. "Ah yes," Geir resumes, "they were tough days." His steely eyes sparkle. "But I am young then, and quickly pick up the lingo."

But what of this place? Geir looks around, waves a hand and talks of Angell. "Ah, he would not recognise what we have become." Geir shakes his head from side to side, looking out to the busy street. "Angell was a rich man, but a man who cared for others. He built this place in 1770, a home for impoverished widows." These days Geir is in his 60s, an odd jobs man, the gardens and buildings his domain.

Back on the street, we glance back to the door now shut, then ahead to the towering cathedral and crypts where the Angell family now abides. Along the north wall we pass ancient elms on lawns of green, sun falling in crooked stripes across shaded tombstones. A young woman in gypsy garb sits cross-legged in our path. Both hands are tightly clasped, fingers and thumbs entwined in a string of beads. A spotted dog lay in threadbare blankets, protruding grey muzzle on a bulging shopping bag; the woman's begging bowl and brown eyes empty.

A student stops, hitching her long skirt to raise a booted foot clear of the frame, propping her bicycle against a tree. Her head is wrapped in paprika scarves, fair hair in Nordic style, braids falling down her back. The similarities between the two are not lost on me, both of similar age, although the student looks confident with her lot. Taking coins from her backpack, the student drops them in the bowl. The beggar's gaze lifts, one hand moving to softly stroke the dog's head. The dog's eyes half open, eyebrows grey, the tail wags.

As we pass, I catch the student's eye and she nods. "You know her husband, he has left her for Poland. She has no home. Everything, it is inside the bag." Dragging the bicycle back to the road, she adjusts her grip and searches for the peddles. She pauses and turns her head towards the beggar. "The dog, you know, I have named her Louise; she is the patron saint of destitute widows."

34

MUSIC, MADNESS AND FAME – Prague, Czech Republic, 2013

On my last night I am dining with Bohdan at the Jindrisska belltower; a rustic restaurant occupying the top three floors. Panoramic views span the famous `one hundred spires'. Just above us hangs the c1518 St Mary's Bell, our tiny table and chairs tucked between great Gothic beams. A flickering candle catches empty pilsner bottles and throws shadows on dark wooden walls. We are eating rare venison in red wine, wild boar, potatoes and asparagus spears.

Bohdan is a busker and a bear of a man; close cropped hair, a still boyish face and an incongruous grey bush of a beard. Most days he drags his cello from near here to Charles Bridge to supplement his modest waiter's income. The faint background music is Dvorak's No8 and I comment on the internationally renowned Czech. Bohdan's right eye flashes. The other, oddly askew and unfocussed, is a childhood re-minder of a Soviet baton and the killings that followed the Prague Spring of 1968.

He shuffles in his seat as the passing waitress smiles. "To be honest", he begins, "I've not much time for the man." He taps the table. "Mmmm... yes, I know there are some that disagree." I press Bohdan for details. "Well, there is no doubt Dvorak was the more...how you say...colourful?" He laughs. "Yes, yes: I know Neil Armstrong took a Dvorak symphony to the Moon! But for me, I am afraid Dvorak rode on the shoulders of Smetana." I'm puzzled, having never heard that name. Bohdan obliges. "A quiet man, his kindness was rewarded by vicious attacks from conservatives." I order a second red, a fine bottle of St. Laurent.

Before leaving, Bohdan signals to the waitress. "Dvorak? I shall show you the difference," he growls. And before long there's a change in the ambience. An opening wavelet of flute is followed by a second, then a pluck of strings. The music swells louder, until bursting into a flood of strings and melancholy. Bohdan talks of history, puffing out his ample chest. "This beautiful piece, it is from the 1870s, but Bedrich Smetana was writing when we rose against the Austrians back in 1848. So...he may not be known to the World, but with we Czechs, it is what is here at home that counts."

The next morning, I wake early to a fog within and with-out; Smetana's life flowing through my scrambled head. The first city bells have already chimed and my split-level pension is quiet as I throw open the bedroom French doors. Outside in the cold morning air, I gulp down a tall orange juice and munch on a piece of dark rye. Thick mist sits in the valley below – a receding river of fluffy powder snow – the monastery bells chiming from beneath onion spires on the green knoll across the way.

With a flight later today, I shuffle down slippery steps and descend the grassy valley amid ghostly black skeletons of trees laden with pregnant blossom buds. At the bottom I enter a walled gateway and emerge to a residential maze of red roofs, rough whitewashed walls, zig-zag streets and lanes. Trams rattle by. I smell pancakes and bacon as commuters and backpackers search out coffee. Across the river Vltava I follow its snaking loops to the last destination marked on my battered map.

A rocky outcrop overhangs the bank. At the top, high spires soar; the past home of ancient kings, and Vysehrad's Basilica of Saints Peter and Paul. I am here to see the graveyard, officially founded in 1869; although some burials are from two centuries before. Stopping by the pantheon I enter and read from a list of names. There's `Antonin Leopold Dvorak'; and I'm surprised to see the now familiar name of Smetana.

The cemetery surrounds are classic art-nouveau. Tall shrubs shade low brick walls among a mosaic of angels and ornate headstones that rise from waves of ivy. The graves of Czech composers commingle with writers, artists and sculptors: there are Kubelik, Capek and Neruda. Here too, are Cech and Myslbek. At Dvorak's grave I peer up at the composer's bust, sitting high on a grand podium ablaze with the great man's name in ornate gold letters of runic form.

When it's time to go, I drop by the grave of Smetana. It's a simple oblong of grey granite with an upright squarish spire for a headstone. There's a plaque with a small star atop the plain printing: `B. SMETANA 1824-1884.' There are fresh flowers; a simple yellow posy and a bunch of jonquils. I look at my watch but pause a moment to recall Bohdan's story.

Although Smetana was a talented child pianist from a well-off Czech family, he struggled and moved to Sweden to make a living as a teacher, choirmaster and composer. His first wife died from tuberculosis after giving birth to four children, with three of those dying in early childhood; his second wife bore him two daughters. Smetana returned to Prague in the 1860s, immersing himself in the city's opera scene. However, at 38 years old he heard voices and the sound of an organ in the everyday rumble of a train. From here he was beset with increasing tinnitus and a deterioration in his hearing. By 1875 Smetana was completely deaf, but somehow embarked on a prolonged period of productivity.

In 1882 he began to suffer imaginary visitors, a distortion of speech and loss of memory. He became more confused and distracted, writing letters to the already dead Mozart and Beethoven. Smetana then became uncharacteristically aggressive, destroying furniture and even his own work. The composer died in the Prague Mental Asylum after weeks of personal degradation and starvation.

My footsteps echo as I wend my way down to the river. I listen to the ripple of white-water and gaze at masses of creepers that hang on river walls. Raising a lukewarm coffee to my lips, bells peel out from the Basilica far above. Could it be? There is no mistaking that melody. It is Bohdan's favourite: Bedrich Smetana's romantic anthem to the Czech nation.

I'm embarrassed at my previous ignorance.

35

MY BROTHER'S KEEPER – Kolkata, India, 2015

Closer to the river, a woman in a full green sari balances a small grotty-nosed child under one arm, and a wide cane basket laden with pots and pans on her head. She chatters instructions to another boy several paces in front. The little guy totes two buckets of water.

Slabs of ghee sizzle and melt in an oversized pan tended by an ancient woman in the brightest yellow. I am in Kolkata, by a Ganges tributary, the air humid and heavy with the smells of cinnamon and asafoetida. I stop in my tracks, the dank river air suddenly caught in my throat. There is a tragic creature on the steps of the ghat and I cannot even guess at his age. His hair is a shock of black, his bent-over form emaciated, his eyes desperately hollow.

I ask Sanjay if anything can be done. He sniffs, my friend's head wobbling from side to side. He shrugs and turns to the now moaning man... or is it some sacred mantra to help him get by? Sanjay's disarming hazel eyes meet mine as he clutches my arm. "It is difficult Sir. Yes, we offer food always. He takes only a handful of rice and will not talk... but am I all my brothers' keeper?"

36

MYSTIC GIFTS – New York, USA, 2014

There is something about these multi-coloured cocoons, the plaque on the wall `Judith Scott: 1943-2005'. I adjust my glasses and lean closer, scratching my head and struggling with the notion of an artist not only deaf and mute, but also stricken with the effects of Down Syndrome. I am in the New Museum of Modern Art (or `MOMA'), New York City, having first dallied outside on the far kerb, staring at this dramatic offset stack of architect-designed boxes – once a parking lot – before braving Bowery traffic; in 1977 the original Tribeca MOMA being the first museum of its kind in this city since WW2. With more adventurous works not so easily accommodated by conventional museums, the MOMA brief to provide an ever changing 'exhibition, information, and documentation centre for contemporary art'.

Mid-afternoon I have first dropped off my coat at reception, gulping coffee from a paper cup and completing a circuit of the ground floor foyer and bookshop; taking in a wall of giant penis's – my Christmas visit coinciding with the exhibition `Hard' – the artist having an interest in the 60s graffiti of men's toilets. With these, the notes say, the artist discovered a window into the male subconscious. I am suddenly feeling a little grubby.

From there I have taken the lift to the top level, the viewing room, clear across The Bowery and beyond, once the seedier southern realms of Manhattan; the plan being to wend my way downwards, taking in each level. At first shocked at the `gritty' 2002 Lower East Side, the architects would later describe their design as a response to that powerful mix; this Bowery incarnation of MOMA opening in 2007; The Bowery said to be the oldest thoroughfare on Manhattan Island.

From the top I've descended to `Come Closer', an exhibition of all things Bowery circa 1969-1989, original artwork and performance documentation by artists with a local connection, a place once considered in urban decline, with more than its share of homelessness and drugs; cheap rent nourishing painters, photographers, filmmakers and musicians. A giant autographed picture of the Ramones stares out from a white wall.

From here it's down another 2-levels and an exhibition `Cosmos', firstly including the primary artist's ceramic work pairing sculptures, the organic subjects of reproduction and replication; the other level devoted to works of wool.

But it's the next level that has captured my imagination,

standing here among Judith Scott's scattered creations; a silent netherworld, oddly primitive – reminiscent of ancient Peru or Egypt – materials determinedly sought out and each abstract shape tightly wrapped: strange mummified bodies of work bound in strands of yarn the colours from some magic rainbow. There is a special intensity, a secret vision I am privileged to be part of, hours of work by a driven artist.

Back at reception I'm bothered by something that won't let go. Jeff hands me my coat. "Judith Scott? Ah yes... of course; be happy to help."

Judith was the twin sister of Joyce, struck down with Scarlet Fever as a kid and losing her hearing. With her deafness undiagnosed, Judith is considered severely retarded and a lost cause. At age seven, her parents – acting on qualified advice – make the difficult decision to send her away.

Jeff stops for a moment; takes a deep breath. "Judith lives in State institutions, separated from family and a loving sister distraught at the loss of her other half." I put my coat back on the bench. "But in 1986, with the death of her father and her mother's breakdown, Joyce worked to become Judith's legal guardian; the sisters reunited after 35-years apart."

"Before long, Judith's enrolled in the Oakland Creative Growth Art Centre, the first in the world to provide studio space for disabled artists." Jeff tilts his head to one side. "But for almost 2-years there's no sign of any artistic interest; until after silently watching the class of a visiting fibre artist one day, Judith is suddenly prompted to start work."

"So that's it", Jeff says, again handing me my coat, "the beginning of the creative explosion you see upstairs; every single piece gathered by Judith, painstakingly wrapped and woven in her own selected colours." Jeff pauses and I wonder how many times he's told the story. "You know… Judith alone decided when the piece was complete." Jeff leans forward as I don my coat. "In some pieces, Judith hid an amulet, the significance only known to her."

Judith Scott worked steadily for 18-years making over 200-pieces, some 3m long, many pieces with a twin, with the complete freedom to use whatever materials she found; her work now all over the world.

In the dark outside, I step carefully on an East Village pavement riddled with ice, still preoccupied with those multi-coloured shapes and Judith's secrets held deep within.

At my apartment steps I wonder at the lot of the deaf and the mute, and philosophical musings that consider the human mind initially void of ideas; a blank piece of white blotting paper, with everything learned as we stumble along. Inside I plug in my notebook and browse the website of Judith and Joyce Scott. There's a quote on the opening page: the words of Art Critic Michael Bonesteel –

"Making something of nothing, or precisely, luring something from the unconscious and giving it material form is the closest thing to real magic in this world."

37

NAUGHTY BUT NICE – Punakha, Bhutan, 2015

A Tibetan baby is born during the 8th cycle of the Year of the Pig. The year is 1455 and his name is Drukpa Kunley. He is a precocious child by all accounts, eventually arriving in Bhutan with his 'Flaming Thunderbolt of Wisdom'. This is 'The Divine Madman' and he shows the Bhutanese how to square one's karma and attain the blissful state of Nirvana.

His days and nights are busy, striking down demons and sleeping with willing young ladies who pay him with beer in exchange for his blessing. The Bhutanese take the stranger to heart, even though a conservative lot and loathed to show affection in public. They paint penises on their homes to protect them from evil spirits, and to promote fertility.

I trudge on towards the temple, where I am told a monk holds a symbolic penis and sanctifies the faithful. Approaching a fairy-tale house, I acknowledge an ancient creature bent under the weight of a bundle of firewood and years of hard labour. She turns stiffly towards me, and scowls from deep within a weathered face. The toothless mouth is tightly clenched, her nostrils flare and sunken eyes stare downwards. She is disgusted with my choice of hiking gear and I am wondering at the inconsistencies of a people that find hiking shorts offensive – shorts that cover my knees – when a mad marauding monk is considered a saint. The woman does not move, but I feel her cold stare follow me as I tread a timeless path by the house, and wonder what curse I have taken on board.

At the end of the house I turn a corner, still struck by that vehement look, until I'm soothed by the sight of a rhododendron forest tumbling off to one side; on the other there's a whitewashed wall, complete with 2-metre upright flying phallus painted in gaudy pink, poking through the coils of a circling dragon.

There is movement up ahead, a young woman carrying water. I blush, but it seems the Divine, the mad and the young are above the earthly emotion of embarrassment, even with me in my bare-legged state.

38

NEW KINGDOM, OLD KINGDOM – Luxor, Egypt, 2017

This is the `Southern Shrine' of the New Kingdom, initially built over 3000 years ago, running from south to north along the River Nile, me peering up at 24m high columns, and the doorway to the Third Antechamber with the Barque of Amun beyond.

In the mist of time, Osiris is the first Pharaoh, the King of the Gods; Seth his brother, but only the God of Chaos and aspiring for something better. Osiris is tricked into laying in a sarcophagus, with Seth filling the box with molten lead and casting the box into the river Nile. Isis is the wife of Osiris and she discovers the box, only to see Seth tear his brother's body to bits, throwing each piece in the river. Isis again rescues her husband, collecting the pieces. She bandages the body back together; all the pieces but one, as the phallus has been eaten by a catfish. The enterprising Isis makes a new phallus of gold, incants a magic spell and briefly brings Osiris back to life. She becomes pregnant and Osiris is transported to the underworld, having now become God of the Dead.

In the cool of the evening modern men lounge on ancient steps dressed in the ubiquitous galabiya and turban. I gaze up to those grand colonnades now glowing gold and ponder the recent discovery of Osiris' final resting place, close by at Sheikh Abd el-Gourna Necropolis.

I wonder at the feelings stirred with a new discovery here, and especially within this Spanish-Italian team when entering a large hall supported by five mighty pillars; the silent walk down a staircase to a dark netherworld and a previously-unknown funerary temple. There's a giant stone statue of Osiris under a high vaulted ceiling; this being the place of final reckoning for those ancient folk – the weighing of their hearts to assess the good in their soul and the weight of their wrongdoings, all before the great God Osiris, now God of the Dead and the Afterlife.

39

ON A LAKE OF TEARS – Halali, Namibia, 2015

In the cool of morning there is a lone giraffe staring this way, the great Etosha Salt Pan his palette backdrop, a 120km blurred horizon. By afternoon we are between sparse breaths of wind: canvas walls and mosquito netting hang limp, the air hot and heavy, the country in the grip of a drought where even good years yield only millimetres of rain. Outside the sun sears salt flats bereft of life, other than a whirligig spiral, a local 'dust devil', twisting north to who knows where, the shimmer of rain a cruel illusion on the distant melting mix of land and sky. My throat is dry.

After dinner and drinks there's the wail of approaching wind, and I wait, until finally it breathes life into canvas walls and mesh windows of this elevated treeless treehouse. Round posts and beam joints creak. Parched decking bakes on connecting wooden walkways that hover high above scatterings of thorn-bush scrub and drifts of white Etosha sand. A pair of black-back jackals follow the stale baked tracks of some death-bent ghost of an animal, maybe a wandering wildebeest, eland or Oryx; an aged, ancient trail hugging this waterless shoreline.

I sleep with the doors open to the silence of the salty pan, but wake to the distant howl of those jackals, and thoughts of a peace-loving people straying this way; those men and children murdered by a tribe of brutal hunters. And I am captive to dark visions of a distraught young woman with a dead child cradled in her arms. She cries in the night until this giant lake fills, awash with the flood of her tears.

40

A PILLAR IN THE STORM – Qal'a Sim'an, Syria, 2015

Noble arches pitch from part-pillars, tumbled piles, broken masonry and rubble; a boulder all that is left of the most famous pillar of all. Saint Simeon moved from a monastery to here for the life of a hermit, living on a 15m high stone pillar. Followers come from far and wide to hear him preach twice each day.

The Saint dies in 459, after 37-years atop his pillar home, the body taken to Antioch escorted by hundreds of soldiers and seven bishops; the pillar now a pilgrimage. Within decades, there are four basilicas, spreading out from a central octagon built about the Saint's famous pillar – the 5th Century Byzantine church perched on a barren knoll of a hill, the ancient city of Aleppo 60km away to the south. In the years that follow there are sieges and earthquakes, uprisings, cholera and Mongol invasions… hundreds of thousands dead.

Here in 2010, black-clad women wander wide dusty paths by walls the colour of sand. Modern ghosts mingle with the old; a rolling timeless desert for all to see. I wonder if the future could be as savage as the past.

41

THE REAL WILD WEST – Vesteralen, Norway, 2013

The narrow road is a roughed-out, potholed track gouged from ragged Norwegian mountains. Winding alongside a grey Arctic Ocean, it is graced with the occasional passing bay and kept in place against northern tempests by discarded mountain boulders.

Turning a last cliffside corner I stop the car and push open the door, buffeted by a wild wind, the dashboard map flying into my girlfriend's face and the door slamming shut against my shoulder. Farther along is a concrete-buttressed causeway snaking its way along the final 100m; an open camping space ahead and across the way a rustic Venetian vision with a Wild West twist.

We have flown 1000km from Oslo to the northern city of Tromso, well inside the Arctic Circle, hiring a car and driving west for six hours via sweeping bridges and tunnels up to 3.5km long; all the way to the Norwegian island of Vesteralen. With Norway's jigsaw geography of bridges, tunnels and skerries, along with the fjords and ferries, it's difficult to tell where the mainland ends and these islands begin. Once home to 1500 residents in the fishing season, the resurrected ghost town of Nyksund, was completely deserted by the late 1970s; the small port deemed obsolete due to its shallow waters and dangerous access.

These days there are about twenty-five permanent residents, due to a 1986 Berlin meeting with a German professor, working with juvenile delinquents facing possible prison. A last-chance offer was mooted, a summer project for two hundred: hands-on clean-up work culminating in a second chance for Nyksund. Two rows of saloon like buildings straddle a dark canal, teetering precariously on grey flagstone sea walls. Crooked facades and narrow wooden wharves gather for mutual support from the raging seas and Arctic winds.

On our first night the air is oddly still; the weather fickle here. Lights from empty upstair rooms escape from small barred windows to throw fiery reflections across the canal. High gabled facades on leaning timber piles cast shimmering shadows that stretch to reach their partners on the opposite side.

Here and there among surrounding mountains, double-storey Shipping News timber-plank cottages go it alone, away from the gaggle of wharfside Nyksund; some perch and prop against impossible rocky knolls, with tie-down cables strung from upper walls to steel pegs rammed into rocky ground.

At the 'living museum' guesthouse Holmvik Brygge, our accommodating hosts are Germans seeking the quiet life – Jasmin here for over 6- years, and Ssemjon for more than a decade. Dinner is a shared tasting plate of smoked seafood: strips of haddock, sea trout and something darker: a cube of whale meat. The Lofoten classic of cod tongues, is lightly doused in flour and fried with flair and a dash of curry; compliments of chef Ssemjon. The crisp German Riesling has a healthy dash of fruit.

"This summer has not been so good," Jasmin confides, "no tomatoes, and the greens so slow." It has been wet for campers too, with many deserting tents for the drier environs of the Brygge, where each rustic room has its own personality. Ssemjon smiles at the mention of weather. When Jasmin first arrived, he worried he may need to lock her up to persuade her to stay. Disparaging Norwegian southerners talk of two seasons up here: the "white winter" and "green winter". Ssemjon's fear proved unfounded – Jasmin loves it all – but she concedes "the white" brings ice and snow to "smooth over the potholes in Ssemjon's road".

In the morning kittiwakes shriek and whistle from the ridges and ledges of long-deserted lofts. Waiting chicks clamber for parents that swoop and soar on their return fly-past from distant feeding grounds. The wind shuffles stacks of loose cladding boards. We breakfast on hard-boiled eggs, toast, cold meats and black coffee, and gaze out the window at Jasmin's "Nyksund television" to ponder the day ahead.

The `Queen's Route' is a 5-hour hike over headland rock, earth, stone and peat, walked in 1994 by Norway's Queen Sonia, taking in the island's postcard mountains tumbling to sea, the sites of ancient AD 750 Viking and AD 1650 Sami settlements. There are bleaker reminders of a 14th century Norway in the ruins of towns decimated by the Black Plague; a time where two-thirds of the population were killed, leaving those remaining depleted and poor; a far cry from the Norway of today.

From Nyksund we walk the causeway, wind at our backs, scrambling up a rambling sheep track; the steep climb rewarded with a view over a Nyksund of matchbox buildings. Mountain sheep with long tails stare with bored eyes, the slippery mud imprinted with many cloven hooves.

Just below the summit of Sorkulen, we pick cloudberries at 450m; something akin to pale swollen raspberries. The ground is hard and stony underfoot, bluebells, sprays of mauve and yellow flowers sprout from sphagnum and moss-laden rock. The curled fronds of shining bright-green ferns seem too delicate for an alpine world.

Across the headland we look down on the village of Langenes, our path again steep and muddy. To the right, low black clouds hang over the tiny church steeple. Inside is a simple wooden frame to which a young girl was once desperately tied then tossed ashore by mammoth waves, the sole survivor of a terrible shipwreck.

From the small fishing hamlet of Sto, we are returning to Nyksund by water. Olaf nods towards a small, bright-yellow inflatable boat hitched to a rickety wooden dock, straining at its rope leash and bobbing with each wave. I look at the billowing grey seas and then at my girlfriend; but it is Olaf's joke. My concerns are dispelled as he points a gloved finger towards a 6m state-of-the-art jetboat with twin motors and two rows of saddle-like seats.

Olaf dresses in the all-weather working gear standard here: a cross between patchwork, multi-coloured overalls and a ski suit. These days he takes tourists on whale and bird safaris and visits nearby skerries. "It has not been a good summer", he reminds us, "lots of rain, with just some baby puffins left." The parent birds having already migrated. "These are the weaker chicks", he says with a resigned nod. "It is the way here; the eagles will have them."

He whistles as we head out, his boat bouncing across choppy waves, "only 1.5m small ones today." He is happy with his lot in Sto, his father and grandfather fishermen; his grandmother once cooking for the fishermen of Nyksund. Olaf's son, too, has chosen a life on the sea. I flinch as cold water splashes across my face and I look up at Olaf. "Some may be 2.5m," Olaf concedes with a chuckle. "Tonight, you shall not be needing salt on your dinner." Our fluoro, sea-survival suits are snug. With an ocean temperature of 12degC, it is a touch warmer than the air that rushes past my ears.

On our last night we are presented with a surprise at Holmvik Brygge: a garnish of Jasmin's first lettuce of a tough summer, and her special apple crumble: her own grandmother's secret recipe, but with a dash of cinnamon. She looks over at Ssemjon leaning by the bar. "Sometimes a little of the new can be good," she says, "but not too much."

42

RIGHTS OF RETURN – New York, USA, 2013

Just off Broadway I'm in a side street by City Hall, the ubiquitous New York crowds somehow missing, the hum of traffic vague and distant. A lonesome monument sits silent and tucked in the shadow of City Planning offices and a thirty-storey Federal skyscraper; that building's construction leading to the 1991 discovery of the largest North American cemetery of Africans and those of African descent. This is a small corner of a much larger 17th and 18th Century 'Negros Buriel Ground', originally 2.6Ha and the resting place of 15000 men, women and children.

With New York's voracious growth, the burial ground was long-forgotten. On this small corner alone, old buildings had been demolished, the ground re-filled and covered with the new; the remains of 419 souls found eight metres below where I stand. With the discovery, all building work here stopped, with a traditional African ceremony to rebury all remains in 2003. Then began the 6-day `Rites of Ancestral Return'; the journey beginning at Howard University in Washington DC, where the appropriate research took place, the procession moving through several major cities and finishing back here in New York; work on this, the African Burial Ground National Monument completed in 2007.

From the street I step past green grass and seven earthen mounds, the reinterred remains; each re-buried in hand-carved mahogany coffins from Ghana, and each lined with African cloth. I stand for a moment by a giant tilted panel in dark grey granite, with the reflection of City Hall, the carved shape of a cemetery guardian, and the words –

For all those who were lost

For all those who were stolen

For all those who were left behind

For all those who were not forgotten

There is another tilted panel behind, forming a roof; shelter at the entry to the libation chamber beneath. A narrow ramp gradually descends to the centre of an open circular chamber, at the depth the remains were rediscovered – the sound of trickling water follows my footsteps – at the bottom the inner circle an earthly map, darker stone on a pale granite disc; the jigsaw of worldly continents. Scribed circles radiate out from a West African epicentre. I stand in the centre reading sentences that straddle an etched circumference, strings of words strangely cold and detached; unknown men, women and children; one recording:

'BURIAL 128 – INFANT UNDER TWO AND A HALF MONTHS'

The women laboured in their masters' homes, the men on heavier work and civil building projects, children indentured from an early age. Lives were short. There was violence. Some died of overwork and malnutrition, others from small-pox or yellow fever. But with colonial laws banning gatherings of over twelve people, funerals were in effect illegal. No ceremonial accounts exist.

But there is dignity in the written reports on the remains found; a small child with a silver pendent around the neck; a string of beads about a woman's waist; bodies in horizontal coffins with the faces up and looking east, in preparation for the next life; burial shrouds and coins gently placed on closed eyes. I read of one man's coffin, with the now familiar heart motif, this time formed with brass tacks and nails on the lid; the West African symbol urging all to learn from the lessons of the past in preparation for the future. There is strength in community, perseverance, sacrifice and respect.

The first settlers arrived in the Dutch colony in 1624 – the Indian island of Mannahatta – the first Africans arriving two years later in chains, from far-flung exotic shores now known as Cameroon, Sierra Leone, Ghana, Nigeria, Mozambique and Madagascar. By 1643, free settlers had arrived from all over the world, already a melting pot of different languages, customs and religions. A French priest claimed to have heard 18-languages on a single occasion, in a settlement of only

500. 'New Amsterdam' was granted the status of a Dutch city in 1653, with the British arriving in 1664 and promptly changing the name to 'New York'.

In 1697 a law forbade any African funerals in the city public cemetery, no matter how small, with all Africans buried north of the city boundary. By the 1720s around a quarter of New York's labour force were slaves. In 1745 the city expanded northwards; with the new city wall bisecting the existing burial ground. Final closure came in 1794, the land subsequently subdivided and sold off for development.

I hear footsteps at the top of the ramp, a stray passer-by; the outer circle a rising path up to the street pavement, with shining steel balustrade one side, low vertical wall on the outside. I run my hand along the face of the perimeter wall as I walk; shining marble, smooth, cold and black, bold African motifs mixed with eerie Manhattan reflections of modern city streetscapes.

43

ROYAL WRECKAGE
– Hampi, India, 2013

Anusha is here every year, and I ask her what drive's her to come so often. She smiles, eyes down. "Life is often hard in India, with office life so mundane. There is sometimes a need to escape, maybe to find some romance." She tosses her long hair to one side and gazes out over the landscape. "Is it not unreal and bewitching?" I nod, following Anusha's gaze over this mighty moonscape alight in rusty, dusty hues, in this land of over 1000 Gods; a land of magic and monkey kingdoms, maybe culminating in this grandly dreamlike but craggy terrain. Giant boulders litter an ongoing undulating plain.

And it's the sacred Hindu text – *The Ramayana* – that immortalizes this place even further, King Rama seeking his kidnapped wife here and meeting the Monkey King himself; *The Ramayama* some 24,000 verses long, an epic Hindu poem in seven books. Anusha says that this was one of the richest and largest cities in the world, capital of the 14th-16th century Vijayanagara Empire. "There are ghosts in this place, in the shadows and in the air."

But all I see is 40degC heat, haze, wreckage and ruins, what's left of over 1600-forts, temples and shrines, pillared halls and gateways, all in pieces after the great Battle of Talikota – a monumental man-made moonscape spread over 4,000 hectares.

44

RUMOURS OF WRONGDOING – Lofoten, Norway, 2012

Cars and trucks wait in orderly lines, the Moskenes-Vaeroy ferry still one hour distant. It is the northern autumn and rain arrives as I leave my car. The church I pass is small, the wet bluestone black. Behind, a mound rises to leaden skies, its sides shrouded in bush and showers of rain. Not far now. My face and hands turn cold.

I am told she tread this very path; with no written record, a young woman from Tennes, near Reine, religious hymns on her lips, tall and straight. In a wedding-white dress, brown hair falls on strong shoulders. I imagine the Arctic air heavy as now, the village folk hushed; their eyes wide and waiting, until startled from the spell they shuffle aside to let her pass. Heads turn, staring, some in denial of what they have heard.

At her trial a judgement was easily made, a punishment to match her crime. There had been celebrations and drinking into the night, her fiancée known as brutal and violent. In a fit of despair, she struck out and killed the man. Arrested and jailed, her life flashed before her eyes, slumped head in hands, miserable and wretched, face wet and smeared. Her mother wept with daughter, shaking her head in disbelief. "But this man of yours, he is surely a bad man, so cold and so cruel." All to no avail, her daughter distraught with some secret guilt. "But mama, you must listen. I am ashamed of what I have done."

A mother always listens. Their faces touched; the words unwanted, white knuckles gripped the daughter's sleeve before desperately pulling away. Could it be her own daughter murdered a baby child? But no, the confession was worse; there were five little ones born in secret, all illegitimate and each killed in turn.

My muddy path is slippery, the rain a soft patter on my jacket hood. My eyes wander back to the fishing village of Sorvagen. The trees sway in a soulful breeze as the car ferry sounds its harbour arrival. From atop the mound, I see the black hull and raised bow. I turn to the church spire, then down at the memorial, the blade of an executioner's axe embedded in stone; the grass green at my feet.

I am among a faceless crowd, mesmerised by a breath-takingly beautiful woman of 44-years; convicted of the most heinous of crimes on the testimony of a heartbroken mother. She calmly kneels, her neck across a wooden block, the gnawing of her conscience finally at rest, long hair brushed aside, hands clasped in prayer. A hooded and leather-clad axeman towers above, an exile from his own country, bare arms raised, axe paused mid-air.

45

SEEKING SHANGRI-LA – The Drakensburg, South Africa, 2014

`.... didn't you ever want to know what was on the other side of the mountain?'

– James Hilton, Lost Horizon.

Funny to find an Antipodean neighbour way out here: a beanie-clad, mumbling, red-head New Zealander in the middle of Africa; him having asked about places I've been, then admonishing himself for being "too nosey".

After only one day, I have realized Keven talks to himself – constantly – the oddball Kiwi banter more rhetorical observation than prying.

From Johannesburg, it's a 200km drive south, meeting `Kiwi Kev' and sharing a room, him with no money, having donated a wallet and sandwich to a marauding baboon; the toothy beast snatching both from the front seat of his van. He had not seen the warning signs: 'You feed em, we shoot em.'

From our overnight digs, I have cajoled my city hire car along potholed mountain roads; Keven's hand-painted van "no good on them hills." At the carpark we have signed a hiker's registration book.

From there it's an hour scrambling over more scoria to get here, on a narrow wandering track cut from the side of stony parapets, all cliff and ragged tumbled rock; my lunch-time goal to sit atop a 3000m high, 5km long, sheer basalt cliff face called 'The Amphitheatre'. We head off once more, to a giant crevasse, a vertical, seemingly insurmountable stone overhang and a pair of rusted chain ladders hanging, hopefully well-anchored somewhere 50m above. Kev gives the first chain a good tug, muttering something about his lack of travel insurance. Atop the second flight I turn around and feel dizzy at the daunting spectacle, and the thought of our return.

It is another hour's tramp across an alpine plateau, once a Dinosaur playground, now vacant and exposed. Finally we stop, Kev taken with green valley views 1000m below, and me with the steep walls of wild rocky ramparts across the way: the once isolated mountain kingdom of Lesotho.

The silence is broken by the chirrup cry of a soaring Black eagle. "Wicked", says Kev, scratching stubbled chin and sprouting whimsical comparisons with the Himalayan magic of Mustang, Bhutan and Tibet. Dragging his eyes from the roundabout wonderland, there is a smirk on that freckled face as he shakes his head and repeats his earlier question; this time definitely meant for me.

The air is cold, the breeze fresh with an increasing chill. There is the zip and rustle of plastic as Kev battles the wrapping on a packet of digestive biscuits. White water run-off gurgles and rushes, hurtling downwards from our stony pews.

I ponder Kev's question, me lost in Lesotho: those distant battlements seeming unreachable. Suddenly I feel Kev's stare. But I keep no tally of peaks or places, these days preoccupied with a lack of time and where I've never been. Kev says nothing at first, nods, shades his eyes and lifts his gaze to follow my own across the way. He looks back at me and squints. It's "Wicked", once again.

Snow drifts lay among wet patches of green lichen, dank pockets and dark crevasses; those castellated walls steep and forbidding, picture-book peaks that hide the great beyond. I'm immersed in a great pondering silence, travelling back to younger days: an often-distant kid in short pants, a faded Lesotho postage stamp, the head of a black man with a feather in his hair, and a dog-eared African map: dreams of a newly independent mountain kingdom. From the kitchen next door, I hear the clink of brown beer bottles on a green-flecked Laminex table. There is the smell of cigarettes and hot popcorn, the gruff banter of a larger-than-life uncle I some-times heard but rarely saw; and late-night tales of a dark and distant continent.

Those dreams drift on the wings of my eagle, my second visit to Southern Africa almost over and having already booked a flight to Lesotho from Jo'burg: that bastion pocket of a country, once the last safe haven in an imploding world, the dream of a visionary village chief who sees the writing on the wall in the early 19th century, leading his harassed people from marauding Zulu armies and encroaching white farmers.

I drag my eyes away, then up to a gathering bank of black cloud. Kev hoists his pack and waves towards the plateau. A rushed march and we reach the ladders; the nimbler Kev dropping over the edge and out of sight. The anchor rods shake, rusted steel scrapes on bare rock and I wait till it stops. I smell burning wood, beans and gravy. There's chatter floating up from far below, the strains of that hybrid Kiwi lilt.

I take a deep breath and am finally on the ladder myself, then a tiny ledge, and the second ladder where I hang mid-air halfway, then down. Kev chats to park rangers with weather-beaten faces and ratty, green overalls; the leader rubbing hands over a crackling cooking fire, antique rifle across bare knees. "Baboons", the one-word explanation.

Back in Johannesburg, I'm waiting for final word on to-morrow's flight; electrical storms and wild winds lash Lesotho and The Drakensberg. It seems I have again missed my chance, the flight cancelled. I wonder if some things are just meant to be: like the chance connection of an errant baboon and a quirky Kiwi called 'Keven'; or a government decree banning climbers from sacred mountains in far-off Bhutan, or even the dashed hopes of an ageing dreamer seeking some impossible Shangri-La.

46

SNOW MONKEYS AND ABSENT FRIENDS – Yudanaka, Japan, 2015

The Tokyo bar is a circle, Teppanyaki hotel chefs in tall hats and shirtsleeves in the centre; their shiny cleavers deftly dealing with slabs of beef, cabbage, prawns and abalone. The air smells of garlic and warm vegetable oil. I sip a Sapporo, the man across the way more intent on his mobile; beside him a woman with a floral print iPad. There is the click and chop of finally-honed steel and the man's fitful coughs, both diners oblivious to the chefs' theatrics. Neither touch their food. The man is around 40 years old, in a heavy winter coat and woollen beanie despite the heating, the woman older.

The next morning, I am at breakfast finishing coffee, when there's a weak voice from the next table. I've been immersed in my paper and a world full of troubles. Initially I don't notice the man from the bar last night, although he's again overdressed with scarf and gloves. The voice is American-English. "You are in Tokyo for business?" he asks and waits for me to answer. I lay the newspaper on the corner of the table and shake my head. I'm here to see the snow monkeys, two hours north of here.

For a moment there's a flicker in the man's watery eyes. He's here for the same reason, to see the most northerly monkeys in the world. "Ahhh yes, sooo special. I've always wanted to see them". He falls silent, sniffs and chews at his lip. "I really must see them." After a time there's a deep breath, a cough, raised eyebrow and finally a smile. "I will see you there." His voice lacks conviction. "The world is small, is it not?" He stares out the hotel window to the coiffured garden. Smokers stand on a red bridge above the waterfall.

There is a deep breath. "I too am smoking far too long". The comment is almost to himself, then his eyes meet mine. "I am often too busy. With business, there is always some emergency in New York or London." He seems anxious, sharp breaths between each sentence. He is in advertising. "There are deadlines, no time for home, no time for any-thing." I push my empty coffee cup to the side, and fiddle with the paper. His skin is grey, the occasional cough more retching than the night before. There is a rash on his neck, and his lower face riddled with acne.

"My sister, she pushes me." There is a pregnant pause. "She will not take 'no' for an answer; wants me to finally meet her son, and yes, see the monkeys; booked the flights, trains and the hotel." There is another cough, and a wan smile. "Her boy is 12 years old already." He makes a move to stand and I offer him my newspaper. He shakes his head. "To be honest, I have no interest in news of the world. We must wish for good weather you and I...a long life, and many monkeys. But I am sorry... I keep you too long. You have a bullet train today." There is a bow as he rises from his table, unleashing another bout if coughing.

From the subway, it's a walk to meet my girlfriend at Central Station, the Shinkansen leaving right on time. The mauve cone of Fuji flashes past, away to the west, framed by Tokyo towers of steel, concrete and glass. From Nagano it's a local train, across orchard flats, then through rolling hills covered in a metre of snow, the bones of plum, cherry and apple orchards.

Our Yudanaka hotel is a 5-minute walk. We book in and leave our bags, the path from the station slippery sludge, surrounding roofs shrouded in thick layers of white. It is a 20-minute taxi to Jigokudani Yaen-Koen – or Hell's Valley – the home of 400 macaque snow monkeys that bathe in the hot springs. The 30-minute path to the steaming springs is steep in parts, winding through a bare, brooding forest, the stone steps steep, the path ice and frozen mud. It is -4degC and I wonder how my Tokyo friend will cope tomorrow. It's two hours before we drag ourselves away from the bathing monkeys, the extended families, mothers and babies.

That night we drink champagne and laze in a steaming

rooftop spa, moonshine aglow on high-pitched roofs. Rolling hills are blue, the ring of mountains black; scattered town lights no match for the endless canopy of stars. Later we dine downstairs, behind paper sliding walls, served by a shuffling woman with a white face, her red kimono a print of camellias and dragons. There are thimble glasses of apple liquor, boiled burdock, littleneck clams and the sweetest Shinshu salmon. A juicy fillet of grilled Shinsyu beef sizzles on a hot stone, along with a dollop of bubbling butter; the wine a local bottle of Hayashi red.

In the morning we sleep late, share a private breakfast, browse the hotel gift shop for bags of jellied cherries and caramelised chestnuts. I hear the phone from reception next door; the answer in Japanese, the hotel owner curt. At the front door he catches my eye and shakes his head. It seems a couple have cancelled late, the woman apologetic. I look over to my girlfriend. Could it be my Tokyo friend?

Outside, icicles hang from hotel fascias and we trudge through powder snow past the deserted station. The centre of town is silent too, wet sidewalks slippery. A man with steaming breath wears a great lumberjack coat, fur cap and ear muffs. He swings a shovel to clear his car. My girlfriend's nose has a tinge of blue.

The road risers by empty hotels, backpackers' digs, quaint Japanese inns and chalets, a wide, white valley away to the west. From valley's edge our goal lay further up the hill – Heiwa No Oka Park, the snow deeper and deeper. The head of the Goddess of Mercy appears suddenly, above the surrounding bones of apple trees and taller outstretched boughs of maple and oak. Covered steps lead upwards from the icy road.

She stands 25m high with a tiara and lengthened ear lobes – on a 3m high podium – left hand raised, the right down by her side. The snow is up to my thighs, a giant bell and temple off to the side. I wonder at the ways of fate, and that enigmatic smile.

In WW2, with Japan in turmoil, the bronze Goddess, or 'Kannon', is cut up and shipped to be scrapped and melted for weapons, part of a last-ditch war effort; only saved by the obliteration of Hiroshima and Nagasaki. Japan immediately surrenders in 1945, the Goddess returned and reassembled.

With the return of the Goddess – now the `Goddess of World Peace' – the park is trio of famous deities are reunited: the Goddess offering the visitor a peaceful life; 'Miroku' the protector from earthquakes; and the 'Tobacco Deity for pro-longing life'.

In olden days, this was a bustling red-light district, each deity visited by prostitutes and locals; cigarettes and flowers offered instead of joss sticks. Later came visitors from the wider area: regular smokers wishing for good health, and those asking for help to quit the habit. Soon, visitors prayed to be protected from cancer, leaving offerings of burning cigarettes.

My girlfriend leaves 100-yen and tolls the bell, a deep ring resounding down the valley, our aim to visit all 3-deities, thereby ensuring our wishes come true. The Tobacco Deity is last, a small stone statue at the bottom of the hill, in a small gable shed open at the front. Small jars hold fading sprigs of mountain flowers.

47

SOMETHING FROM NOTHING – Doha, Qatar, 2015

With Qatar summer temperatures between 40-50degC, I set out in the early evening from the seething stalls of Souq Waqif, dodging freeway traffic and heading down a grand palm-lined avenue to the Islamic Museum of Art, a stepped limestone vision alight and afloat the Arabian Gulf. A space age skyline beckons across the bay.

Adama is a journalist, chats with a cultured London accent, with dinner a white-linen affair atop the Museum. We drink from an icy-cold crystal carafe of grape, cranberry and litchi juice blended with raspberry, lime and honey. In deference to the museum, there's no alcohol here. There is house-made bread, plates of roasted hammour with soft and crunchy rice, French snails and a vegetable salad with za-atar dressing. Over thimbles of sweet coffee, we are offered roasted apricot and Iran pistachio ice-cream. The vision is French, the flavours straight out of Arabian Nights.

Early morning, I wander the famous 5km Corniche promenade, arguably the oldest landmark here, the museum already lost in haze, a warning of the heat to come. The plan is to again meet Adama, and I gaze past painted dhows and across to that iconic glass and steel skyline; the rows of dhows a hint of the innocuous fishing village Doha once was.

Adama is talkative, me already sweating and the air-conditioning pumped up to full. He is late, having stopped for fuel, and I am surprised at the size of his car – a large black European people-mover – but he smiles and drops his foot to the floor. "No problem. A Big Mac will cost me more than to fill the tank." He continues. "Yes, life is good here. We have a high standard of living, and the best healthcare. We have education and sustainable development." He smiles, revealing brown teeth. "We have singing sand dunes and a hospital for falcons!" I get the picture; there is everything here.

"Qatar is the biggest exporter of natural gas." He says. "We have the fastest growing economy in the world, the greatest wealth per capita. You must see our football stadium." I am told Qatar will be the smallest country ever to host the World Cup, the building holding 80,000 people. We pass sandpit construction sites, the great shell of the National Museum, a sea of steel frames wave upon wave, evoking memories of the Sydney Opera House immersed in unruly stacks of broken plates, Doha a melting pot of architectural ambitions with many construction workers killed in accidents.

Adama's car speeds down a wide road baking and bereft of pedestrians, somehow oddly empty despite the traffic but crowded-in by eclectic towers of twisted steel and glittering glass; these odd shaped offices and shopping centres, Qatar's commercial centre. I'm captivated by the forest of fairy-tale towers flashing past, and Adama's bloodshot eyes lift to catch mine in the rear-view. "You know the meaning of `Doha'?" I shake my head and he laughs. "It comes from the Arabic 'Ad-Dawha', meaning 'the big tree'."

I ponder the miracle of time, this place once all sand, a rustic fishing village surrounded by `singing' dunes... and one big tree where there is now a forest of glittering towers.

48

SUNSET SPIRES – Bagan, Myanmar, 2015

With our last night, it's another sunset skyline of spires, heat and haze: 3000-temples and pagodas built between 11th and 13th century, some say deserted by a Myanmar king. We've wandered these baking plains with a battered map, from one group of soaring spires to another, lost but not lost; bouncing on electric bikes across hot asphalt and rutted sand tracks.

Better known temples have troupes of artisans, traders and mild-mannered touts; inside – the worshipped, the worshippers and monks, crowds of the curious and the seekers of something. Most are more isolated, lonely buildings, an escape from the heat through darkened doorways to hallowed halls and walls, the imbedded memories and shadows of those that came before.

49

A TALE OF THREE CITIES – Soweto, South Africa, 2013

It is early morning, The Healer a tall woman with the short-cropped, knotted hair of her people. I lean closer to hear her words; those bloodshot eyes blurred but vacant. She talks of `home' and the importance of family, before suddenly falling silent. We're standing on an elevated ancient seabed: the rocky ridge of Johannesburg's Melville Koppies; at our backs the distant towers of Jo'burg proper.

The temperature drops, across the way the rolling urban hills of Sophiatown: these days neat, quiet houses and gardens, tarred roads and pale rendered walls, first surveyed in 1903, an urban experiment with black Africans owning property and living among other races. With the distance from

Johannesburg and a sewage plant built nearby, most whites had left by 1920.

By the late 40s, Sophiatown included 54000 Black Africans, 3000 Coloureds, 1500 Indians and 686 Chinese; the violence, jazz, poverty and politics, all home to writers and artists, but far too close to circling white suburbs. With a National Party election victory in 1948 and the Immorality Amendment Act of 1950, mixed races would no longer be allowed to live together.

The Healer sniffs... then coughs. A morning breeze chills my face as I rub my hands and stuff them deep in down jacket pockets. She lifts those bloodshot eyes, her breath already beery. She talks of a terrified 5 year old in 1955, arms wrapped tightly around a mother's knees. There is no tomorrow; the pre-dawn icy cold, the nightdress flowery but thin, cold rain on bare arms. The Healer sighs, looks up and shivers; the little girl's sick with German measles. 2000-police roam Sophiatown, guns, rifles and whips in hand. Straining dogs on taught leashes snap and growl, gunshots crack; family furniture tipped in the back of police trucks, driven south 35km and dumped. The human relocation to Soweto follows, the fractured families dazed and silent. I gaze southward to the distant desolate profile of a gold tailings dump. Over the next 8-years Sophiatown is bulldozed, flattened and obliterated from South African maps.

Late afternoon I am alone, standing on a Soweto mound at the base of a circular tower in the centre of a park; the surrounding gardens a breath of fresh air, the tower built from cast blocks from the ashes of Sophiatown, a dark rough grey, smudging the sleeve of my jacket. I'm struck by the quiet. The iron-barred gate is narrow, squeaks and opens with a stiff push. I head up a flight of winding uneven steps. At the top I blink, the sky a washed blue, then turn to peer over the wall and get my bearings, momentarily mesmerized by the crow of a rooster and the rows of houses stretching towards the horizon.

Along gravel footpaths by traffic-choked streets, I pass impromptu fruit, trinket and sweet stalls; friends ambling in fits and starts, a frail old woman balancing a bulging green bag on her head while Friday groups of youths lean on parked cars and swig from brown bottles of beer. Packed minibus taxis prop at corner pick-ups and awkward angles, to fit in one more fare. I slide open the door with a loud bang, scramble up the back – me a lone white face – swapping greetings with Soweto folk and squeezing between a nurse and a doctor. My fare is cheerfully relayed by willing hands to the Zulu driver up front, my change returned the same way.

I'm met at my accommodation gate by The Healer; gazing down the end of the road at the daunting vision of the mine tailings dump looming close by and skyward, aglow in the orange and red of a dying sun but loaded with lingering traces of arsenic once used for the extraction of gold. The Healer lives in a room out back, this rambling house home for an extended family of twelve. She smiles wanly after a meal of pap and gravy: the local polenta staple of corn maize. I am a guest, she says, as she wipes her mouth. I can borrow her bed for the night. For a moment I stand peering through the 60cm square, cell-like window, through pretty lace curtains.

Reaching for my pack, my once black shoes are all dust. I tug at the bolt, push the door, step up and inside.

There is the faint smell of lavender. The Healer's room is small; narrow bed pushed against one wall, the window directly above, the floorspace all of 2m square. A brightly coloured quilt lay neatly folded, a small wreath circle of dried mountain sage neatly sitting on top; the pillow at the far end, frilly pastels of pink and blue. There is no room to move; the box fridge, microwave and polished ply bench all in the compact alcove of a built-in wardrobe. A vase of freshly gathered flowers sits on the bench; a small framed picture of a young schoolgirl, staring up at a woman in a 1950s bonnet, tall and straight in her Sunday best. By the photo there's a small glass orb on a plastic base; a cottage inside, a layer of snow on the steep gable roof.

I choose to sleep on the floor, tucked between the fridge and bed. The night's freezing; there's no insulation here. I cross thermal-clad arms, woollen beanie pulled on tight, down jacket thrown across cold knees. The Healer has a sister and three brothers. The sister has a daughter named Marcia: a sweet 19 year old with an infectious giggle and a shining round face. I ask about The Healer and Marcia drops her eyes.

It seems The Healer is special: the neighbourhood's conduit to ancestors and full-time carer for a bedridden mother; washing, talking, changing bedding and bedclothes, the old lady's face gaunt and grey, the smile warm but weak. Of the brothers, one runs the beer-house out front, the local she-been, the single room bare except for a squarish table with a plastic top, a bench seat and two rough-carved chairs. He sleeps next door, by a beer fridge that rattles and hums day and night.

I drink outside, in a small paved yard among neighbours and passers-by. The Healer stands in the shadow of a wall just watching, quietly coughs and demolishes a pack of cigarettes, until finally emerging and drawing close. All banter stops, The Healer saying nothing at first; just looks me up and down and refusing to leave my side. I feel all eyes on this woman, some wary, some in awe, whispers and nods as if all but me understand.

In the morning things are slow and I'm leaving but am suddenly swept up in the arms of The Healer. Her talk is excited and scattered, slurred words I just can't catch. I look around for help, young Marcia gripping my elbow and nodding. "She is saying you must visit your mother." Marcia's voice is hushed. "She is telling you it is time."

Those bloodshot eyes are wide, The Healer nodding her head until finally releasing her grip. I am followed to the kitchen where I buy The Healer a morning bottle of beer; Marcia's mother, The Healer's sister, stands at the stove, solid churchgoing stock, scowls and raises her eyebrows. The money is snatched from my hand and tucked in a jam tin by the fridge. "You must not be taking notice of such talk," she grumbles. The Healer refuses to let me leave without me promising to ring.

Back at my apartment, my pack lay open on a waist-high bench, me pulling out empty chocolate wrappers and a sweat-stained shirt. I am about to email `home', the whisky bottle half empty and visits to far-off Melbourne less frequent these days. There is a tap on the tiled floor: a torn-off piece of beer-carton cardboard with a note scratched in a shaky hand. Bending down, I screw up my eyes; the name and phone number almost unreadable.

I recall The Healer, the concern written on her pock-scarred face. I must go to my mother, she had said: a mother who stepped out in front of a car to be instantly killed some forty years ago; me having never visited the grave.

50

THE TALE OF A TWISTED CROSS – Berlin, Germany, 2013

From my Mitte hotel in what was once `East Berlin', I wander towards Nordbanhof and along Bernauer Strasse, a onetime frontier street on the Cold War border between East and West. I climb a viewing platform and gaze across to a reconstructed guard tower from another time, and a strip of green lawn, once a no-mans'-land squeezed between two walls and barbed wire. This is what's left of `The Wall': a renovated portion of the `real' wall, barb wire and a death-strip, no-go area to dissuade anyone contemplating escape to the West. Approximately 1000-graves were exhumed and relocated from here.

The story begins in 1945 at the end of desperate WW2

street fighting. Bernauer Strasse pre-empts the coming of yet another war, a `colder' war. This street follows the front of buildings on the East Berlin Soviet side. Barriers are erected and many residents spontaneously flee. The West Berlin Fire Department hold rescue nets at street level, as East Berliners slide down ropes. Some jump, with many hurt. The first Cold War fatalities occur. The buildings are evacuated after The Wall is built, anyone left on the east side forced to resettle elsewhere, windows and doors bricked up. The population continue to rebel against the new barriers. There are protests and escape tunnels dug.

I walk further along, to the `The Window of Remembrance': a montage of faces of those that died and were buried in this death strip no-man's-land. There are 138, their names, birth and death dates, each victim individually commemorated here; all having died at The Wall by accident while trying to escape, or shot dead.

And there was once a church here, an imposing building having survived WW2 but in 1945 finding itself in the Soviet Sector. With the Berlin Wall built in 1961, it ran directly in front of the church on its western French side, but behind it on the eastern Soviet side. The church was left within what was an almost inaccessible death strip, with most of its Parish in the neighbouring French Sector. Soviet guards used the tall church as a vantage point. Attempted escapes from East to West were rewarded with the order "shoot on sight".

From the grass, I walk to a wooden monument. The initial church foundations all that's left now, the church having been fitted with explosives, blown apart and demolished in

1985 by the East Germans, 'to increase the security, order and cleanliness on the state border with West Berlin'. The cross that had stood at the top of the steeple was gone.

Only 4-years later the first section of The Wall fell on the night of November 10, 1989, pieces knocked down between Bernauer and Eberswalder Strasse to create a new crossing between East and West Berlin. The official overall demolition began in June 1990, with the Berlin Wall Memorial placed here. A wooden structure is the new chapel built over the foundations of the sanctuary of the previously destroyed church; oval-shaped, rammed-earth, the inner room encircled by vertical wooden columns with gaps to allow light. The core of the chapel is orientated eastwards.

But it is the original church cross that brings me here; the very cross that once stood at the top of the 1894 neo-Gothic steeple, then somehow disappeared. The great cross now sits on this concrete slab out front of the wooden chapel monument, its form twisted, rusted and contorted, having broken off the spire with the impact of the explosion and being subsequently hurled to the ground and quickly hidden by East German cemetery workers until The Wall finally came down 5-years later.

51

TOPKNOTS AND TALKING STONE – Easter Island, Chile, 2013

I am met at the airstrip by Toi my guide, with a vice-like handshake and a welcoming lei of yellow bougainvillea draped around my neck. Two skinny girls in grass skirts and goosebumps serenade to the strains of a ukulele played by a man in a knitted jacket over an Hawaiian shirt. It is winter on Easter Island. Toi's home is on the coast, by the main village of Hanga Roa. He swaggers around his clapped-out Kombi, kicking tyres with dusty sandaled feet. "The roads, they are no good here. I must be checking for tomorrow."

That night we walk a beach strewn with stranded sea

cucumbers and mounds of fresh kelp. Toi talks of `his' people. The air is still and southern stars line a curved horizon. These are the same constellations that guided the ancient mariners of the 5th century; aided by swell, the winds and the great god Make Make. Mainland Chile lay 3000km to the east and Pitcairn Island 2000km westward.

My guide is a restless soul with a mop of ragged red hair that sits in a topknot like some of the enigmatic statues here. He is hazel-eyed, tall with muscle upon muscle. Tattoo stripes peek from his polo shirt collar and travel up to square set jawbones. He is happy riding his horse and "doing the occasional guide thing". And there's a tourist market where he helps his mainland artist girlfriend and chews the fat with Rasta friends.

In the morning we leave the village in the Kombi, passing a 4m upright statue, a local moai with arms down, rigid at his sides. He stands alone and forlorn with his back to the sea. The wide, furrowed brow tops a long bridge of a nose. Toi twists in his seat and whispers. "Within each lives the spirit of a mighty chief. He is a much-loved brother, a father or uncle." I wonder where his bones may lie.

The Kombi rattles and shakes across a mostly forlorn landscape, passing a scattering of Australian eucalypts. I am in the middle of an island almost treeless, the palm and sandal-wood forests long gone. We jump out and I am struck by the quiet as we pass another moai – fallen this time – the first of many I see. My boots slip in rubble and clouds of dust catch in my throat. Another statue is 3m tall, although buried to his shoulders in the scoria of a crumbling volcano. He has a slight backwards lean and a skywards-tilted nose as if sniffing at the salty air. Long ears hang to the ground from a narrow flat-topped head, and I run my hand across a weathered shoulder to find chiselled `tattoos' at the base of his neck.

Back at Toi's place we sit in darkness, sharing mashed bananas and pumpkin wrapped in banana leaves and eating ceviche with our fingers. Tonight, there is an increasing chop in the Pacific swell, the broken surface catching silver chards of a waning moon. Toi clears his throat and blows streams of smoke from his nose. "I will tell you what the moai tell me *Senor*."

Toi is a master, his tale ebbing and flowing like the sea. I hear the splash of oars; chants and shouts from brave folk I cannot see, the melodic singing of women. Broken streams of phosphorus trail behind mighty double-hulled canoes with tall prows; bound together with braided coconut fibre, cracks sealed tight with the sap of breadfruit trees. They arrive with taro and sugar cane. There is breadfruit, giant bunches of bananas, coconuts, gourds and sweet potato. As with all their epic journeys, they come with pigs, dogs, chickens and rats.

But this place at the end of the earth, is unlike any other; with coral at ragged cliffs in fits and starts, there's no lagoon to stop the often-monstrous waves. On cold nights pandanus-leaf shelters blow into the sea, leaving flimsy bark capes flapping on wet skin.

Toi pauses, rolling another spliff. "This is no tropical paradise *Senor*. There are few plants and animals. Not everything will grow." He turns his head from side to side. "Look around you *Senor*, the island, it is volcanic. The fresh water, it is only in the volcano calderas."

Before long there are only chickens and sweet potatoes left. Eventually there are 300 stone platforms around the island, called 'ahu' and dedicated to Toi's ancestors; each with a row of up to 15 stone moai, overlooking huts shaped like boats. And now there are 600 unfinished moai scattered about the volcano quarry. Some moai and ahu are from the 8th century, with most erected between the 11th and 17th. "But there is a problem *Senor*," Toi continues. "There are between fifty and one hundred warriors needed to drag each moai into place. There are many wooden rollers needed; and soon, no trees are left for the fishing canoes. Then the crops, they fail." Toi smells the air. The wind is turning, with waves heaving and crashing like dominoes on the beach. The wind tinkers with the corners of Toi's rusty iron roof and we move inside.

The story continues. "With the forests gone, the birds desert us. They no longer come here, roosting only out there," Toi waves a tanned and tattooed arm, "on the most dangerous rocks." Toi goes quiet, passing a bottle of *pisco*. I take a swig, the woody sweet fumes going straight to my head. Toi smiles, then frowns. "Civil war comes and the moai are all toppled, except for those unfinished."

Vicious wars continue into the 19th century, with survivors living in caves and resorting to cannibalism. Toi takes another puff and clears his throat. "Families, *Senor*, now they cower in holes. We do not do so well here, spoiling the land and living like savages. We gnaw on the bones of neighbours."

Toi leans forward. "This is not the Polynesian way *Senor*." The wind howls and rattles the iron roof as Toi exhales another cloud of smoke. "We lose our connection to the land, and we forget *Senor*, we are only the keepers of the land for our children."

52

TOUCHING THE SKY – Granada, Spain, 2013

I meet Candelaria at a café on the slopes of the Albaicin – the old Moorish quarter – and sip peppermint tea from petite porcelain cups. She orders almond cookies and apologises for her Spanish. The courtyard is open, with large paved flag-stones, the tables squarish, small and scattered. Surrounding high walls on three sides are alive with masses of espaliered red roses. We sit soaking up the last of the sun, gazing east-ward over receding terra cotta rooves as they disappear from view down to the winding river realm of the Darro. Across the river lay slopes cloaked in the green of lush gardens, up to the rising knoll and already russet-tinged walls of the Alhambra citadel; once home to 13th and 14th century Moorish rulers.

Candelaria, a mosaic artist, suggested this café to watch the sun set over the Alhambra. She has shining eyes to match her name, dark olive skin a startling contrast to the white of a simple linen blouse; a bright embroidered mantoncillo casually draped over her shoulders. We are chatting of Washington Irving's `Tales of the Alhambra'; Irving an American writer `spellbound in the old enchanted pile' of a dilapidated Alhambra when living there in 1829. Her eyes widen as she flicks the pages. "Ah, yes; a wonderful read. My son knows all these stories." She gently rests my book on the table and looks up. Like Irving, Candelaria is captivated by Andalusia, its exotic mix of the Moorish and Gothic. But she tells me, it's this place, the Albaicin, where the magic truly lay. "And to be finally actually living here is a dream come true... like coming home in some strange way." Candelaria looks wistful, eyes half-closed in thought.

Leaving Candelaria, I follow once-secret stairways and paths downwards, the Albaicin's arabesque labyrinth of narrow streets winding hither and thither: Candelaria's new neighbourhood. The rambling maze of whitewashed walls are tea houses, terraces and town houses mingled with timeless, courtyards and cobble-stoned lanes revealing occasional glimpses of distant citadel lights that flicker in the dark. At the bottom I follow the Carrera del Darro, passing crooked walls along a winding river, by narrow stone bridge arches bathed in the golden glow of street lamps. Then it's up another cobbled path, the Cuesta del Rey Chico, and another 15-minutes to my Parador room.

In the dark I imagine this citadel in Irving's day: walls on the verge of collapse, columns in disrepair, rooves leaking, a crumbling tower home to tenants living with bats and owls; washing hanging from every opening. One ragged creature claims royal heritage; another is a small fairy of a thing, living beneath a stair. She has outlived 5-husbands, is a master of needlework, sings and tells odd stories; where she is from no-one knows. There is a man with a bottle nose and a cocked oilskin hat; Irving living among a family with lineage traced back to the 15th century; their poverty handed from father to son.

Irving himself was born in New York, 1783. It is very late, and at the open window I inhale the sweetness of orange blossom. The falling waters of a fountain sparkle, the splashes soft and enamouring, the edges of hallways and marble columns lit with moonshine. I read of Irving, him lulled to sleep by the distant serenade of an ancient guitar, the echoes of castanets and the swish of some Spanish dancer's dress.

In the morning, the summer light shines on citadel walls and marble columns, royal surrounds now anything but dilapidated and Irving's squatter companions long gone. Grand stalactite cupolas vie with ornamental works in stucco, ceramic tiles brightly coloured, precious wood skilfully sculptured, Alhambran palaces, guard room, patios, exotic fountains and gardens. To the east lays the rural residence; the most resplendent gardens and water features dominant over summer houses and pavilions. For here it's the giant boxwoods that set the mood; along with carnations, roses, willow and cypress. The Court of Lions has the stillest water in wide basins, gently falling, eventually gliding through narrow canals, and exploding into jets and cascade falls.

From there I amble 100m to a quaint 3-storey building, the Hotel America; cream stucco, bougainvillea-draped wrought-iron balconies and window boxes. Built at the beginning of the 14th century, the courtyard, southern aspect and garden are classic urban Spain. I breathe balmy summer air seated among blue-tiled tables. Candelaria is late and my mind wanders. There, in a leafy corner across the way: can I see the 36 year old Irving? A handsome man by all accounts; tall, in the elegant Western attire of the times, dark curling hair, aquiline nose, and white ruffled shirt under a dark jacket. He's holding court drinking Barbadillo and picking at a bowl of green olives.

With Candelaria's arrival we talk again of Irving, and she smiles when I change the subject. Yes, she is Australian, from my home city as it happens and her family emigrating in the early 60s, working hard in her uncle's Melbourne restaurant. I'm incredulous at her not having spoken Spanish at home, and she shakes her head. "Sadly no. I'm so sorry now, that I paid so little attention to the language. But I was young, and I was Australian. I listened of course, and spoke a little. Away from the restaurant I was embarrassed. At school I would never speak Andaluz. All the kids knew me as `Candy', my twin sister `Mary'." Candelaria shrugs. "In my 20s I did try to learn, but my husband saw no point; and suddenly I'm a mother!"

I offer sangria from my carafe, but she refuses then smiles. "I must pick up Mama and my baby from the airport. He's eight now." I ask about Candelaria's parents and she hesitates. "Ah, my father, he hates me being here." She stares down on the tiled table. "He tells me he sees his dead father every single day, and Franco's brutal murder of Lorca." Candelaria raises her ample eyebrows, and I take her point; I know the great Andalusian poet. She nods and continues. "Well, my father idolises Lorca."

" I remember when I said goodbye, my father, he tells me that in Spain, the dead are more alive than anywhere in the world – that's Lorca. Father tells me he can never forget." Candelaria's eyes well up with tears. "Mama cried when I applied for the visas." Candelaria pulls out a handkerchief and blows her nose. "She has been so kind, and will cry much more when she says goodbye." Candelaria hesitates for a moment. "My father, he does not understand; says I'm being selfish to take his only grandson. Siss agrees." Candelaria takes a deep breath. "I just need to spread my wings."

I think I understand, and recall Irving's regrets when called back to New York's 'bustle and business', while wondering how he would ever '...endure its commonplace, after the poetry of the Alhambra?'

53

TOWERS CASTLES AND KANE – New York, USA, 2013

It is the 1941 film `Citizen Kane' that brings me here, just south of Columbus Circle; to a castle of a place built in 1928 for William Randolph Hearst's publishing empire. Hearst was a powerful man with a thing about castles it seems, his newspapers read by one in four Americans and at the time already owning a twin-towered Mediterranean castle in California. The young director Orson Welles was about tearing castles down, producing the film Citizen Kane; a thinly veiled biography of Hearst.

It is 4pm, already dark, and with head down I push through sheets of rain. Shoppers rush this way and that, water thrown up from passing streams of New York cabs; yellow flashes on wet roads dappled with reflections of car and Christmas lights. Irate drivers sound their horns. This castle entrance is flanked by columns; statues of Comedy and Tragedy on the left, Music and Art on the right. There are other figures outside too; Sport and Industry, Printing and the Sciences. It had always been Hearst's intention to add a tower here, with formal plans filed in 1946 but never acted upon.

Throwing myself into the warmth of enclosed revolving doors, I pull my hood away from my face. I squint. The interior is bright and I am greeted by a trim man in a dark suit, mobile at his ear; my eyes drawn to the lipstick-red rosebud pinned to his lapel. He looks up briefly as I motion to him; "No Sir, you definitely cannot go up the escalators!" Taking off my wet jacket I try to shake the cold from my blue fingers; feeling small on the spacious lobby floor of polished flagstones, the original building gutted to leave the castle shell only. I am stunned as I look up, Hearst's longed-for tower rising way above me. From the floor, three escalators climb amidst a sculptured waterfall extending across the width of the building; fifty tonne of glass panels. Above that, a 21m high vertical fresco of Hudson River mud.

Would this have satisfied Hearst? He was certainly not impressed with Citizen Kane, having tried to stop the film's release and offering to pay for the destruction of all prints. Orson Welles refused, with Citizen Kane praised for its narrative, innovative cinematography and music score; and subsequently voted one of the world's greatest films. I have slept through the middle twice, but still wonder about the `rosebud' finish.

Looking outside, the rain has stopped. I have been in

here for an hour and leave through the same revolving door. Things are not as frenetic now, for 8th Avenue that is, with me standing in the centre of the footpath and leaning back. I crick my neck, taking in the new forty-six storeys; this 182m, diagrid framed, all glass and steel; a dramatic vision for the modern headquarters of the now global Hearst Corporation. I'm not too sure what William Randolph Hearst would have made of all this, but I'm thinking it may have helped the film.

54

TRAVELLERS LOST – Uis, Namibia, 2017

I am in Namibia, on the edge of the 2000km Namib Desert, the oldest in the world I am told and 350km northwest of the once colonial centre of German West Africa, Windhoek. From the setting sun my gaze drifts north and way down to the road at the toe of this great tailings hill. The air is finally cool after the burning African sun, the earth still hot under my sandaled feet. Across the road is the hamlet-town of Uis – or `Bitter Water' – once with a population of 3600 souls but downgraded to a mere `settlement' in 2010.

Away to the west is The Skeleton Coast, littered with the bones of forgotten mines and over 100-shipwrecks on a desolate coast. William says this is a land of "forgotten enterprise, of failed dreams, lost lives… and many stories." He is brown, tall and rakish, but drags one leg that reminds me of the ravages of polio. His face has the scars of tribal initiation or maybe some African childhood ailment; his eyes blood-shot but alert. He talks of work. "Not so good Sir, work is a problem here. Not so many jobs..."

But something has broken my friend's train of thought, his soft voice trailing away to nothing. He stares down the straight strip of a road to the western end of Uis and I follow his line of sight. I see only dust and desert scrub. William's outstretched arm and finger reveal no more, but I am told there are eleven unmarked mounds down there, somewhere. Try as I may, I can't see a thing from way up here.

Uis is a mining town, or once was, and the world's big-gest tin mine. I turn from the neat cluster of distant town houses and street trees below, to back behind me: a gaggle of roofless empty shells, what is left of the mine buildings nestled between the folds and valleys of these moonscape mountains of tailings. With a fall in the price of tin, the mine shut in the early 1990's, the 3600 inhabitants leaving and the `village' officially downgraded to a `settlement', then more recently bought lock-stock-and-barrel by a South African businessman.

Where we stand is the top of a single white dune that towers over all the others, a familiar landmark in these parts. With the red glow of the sun finally finished, we head down a curving, breakneck road; on one side a man-made cliff. My clapped-out pickup brakes squeal, and the gears clunk. I pull at the wheel this way and that. Talcum-like dust clouds leak inside and catch in my throat. At the bottom we cross the main road to a great crater of a hole. William tells me the tin was taken from here, the man-made abyss now filled with water – oddly incongruous in a fearsome dry land of endless straight roads.

William lives alone in the old African 'township' just east of Uis `proper', a dusty segregated legacy of apartheid days. He is quiet for a guide, works 2-weeks on and 2-weeks off. He shares the job with others, "Jobs are precious here... always have been." He travels by donkey and cart 50km to his mother's and family's village weekly, rainbow-coloured but rusted tin sheds that sit in the shadow of the Brandberg, the highest mountain in Namibia, and a special place where over 2000 prehistoric paintings lay tucked in ragged nooks and crannies.

"The Germans 'discover' the paintings in 1918, but there is no respect here." William shakes his head. Those eyes narrow. "*Ja...* you splash your Coca Cola on the most famous... `The White Lady'... to see the painting better with your white eyes...and this painting, he is fading with the years... for `he' is not a lady, but a shaman." William purses his lips. "But your eyes see what you want to see. And the damage, it cannot be fixed."

William places a hand on my shoulder, and there is just the hint of a smile. "Our people know of these paintings of course Sir...for over 20,000-years. But for your people, they are new." His eyes meet mine and he shakes his head. But William is optimistic. He must be, he says. He has three kids. He sees a future in welcoming worldly but wayward tourists like me. There are now hot air balloon rides to take in the rugged expanse of this place, and the tourists want to see the desert elephants that follow ancient winding riverbeds. And William knows how to find them. These elephants are different he says. "They are in small groups only, digging for water. The legs are longer than other elephants because of the distance they must travel to survive." He nods when I ask if he would show me. "*Ja...* we may be lucky Sir", he says.

Next day I try my luck with William. I stop my pickup in the dry reverbed sand and lower the air pressure so as not to get bogged. William asks a goat herder of the animals' whereabouts. The friend is a young boy in a denim jacket with a wooden staff and dazzling white teeth. He has seen our elephants, pulls a mobile from his pants pocket, stands on one leg and leans on his staff while phoning on ahead. He nods as he talks, and William interprets. Yes, they are travelling east. "Sir... not far now."

Hours later we catch them, firstly a lone bull, with William raising both hands and signalling for me to stop; very respectful and insisting we keep our distance. "These bulls, they can be angry for no reason...they are old Sir. Last year we have some trouble here, with a car bonnet crushed for no reason." William watches the bull closely, falling silent. There is a rare grimace from the side of my friend's mouth. "The German tourist...he was not so happy with the elephant sitting on his Mercedes." We wait for the animal to move safely off to the side.

Around yet another bend, we are surprised to come across two fully-grown females in the fading afternoon light, just over in the bush, not ten metres away, and one young calf tucked between. My luck has held good and we watch for an hour until they disappear in the dark.

In the morning I drop by the African township store and buy some kids' clothes from a Chinese trader; a parting gift for William's family. I leave them with a friend of William's who runs a hot air ballooning business in Uis, and then head for The Skeleton Coast.

At the edge of town there's a cloud of dust as I pull over and gaze back at the flickering town lights for one last time. I wonder if this is the place and wander off the road in the gloom until I see the mounds. Yes, there are eleven; simple graves, the occasional stone, the earth bare and red. There is an ominous silence here. Surrounding sentinels are clumps of Melkbos; a Namibian bush of tubular grass-like uprights, the central stump of a trunk hidden somewhere within. I stare down at the mounds and walk to the nearest bush where I break off a frond that bleeds milky latex ooze between my thumb and forefinger.

William had said: "Where these men set camp... this bush Sir, it is not so good. *Ja*...if you break it, you must not have any cut or scratch. Some animals, they eat the tips... it is messing the brain. The first people here, they use for the poison arrows, but must always be cutting away the bad meat." William waved a finger in front of my face. "They must not be eating this meat." I shake my hand to try and rid myself of the sticky mess, then wipe my fingers in the red sandy dirt. I rub more dirt between my hands until the stuff is finally gone, then wipe the hand on my pants. At 2m high, these plants are food for Oryx and rhino, but apparently for nothing else.

My eyes are drawn back to the graves, my thoughts to William's sombre face and words. "These young men... for them also, life is hard. They leave their families up north to travel here for work that is not real. They survive by hunting local game."

William filled in the gaps where he could. In the early 1900's, two carloads of Ovambo men are away from home, having driven over one thousand kilometres from some-where up north; maybe from the steaming jungles of Caprivi, or the desolate desert country of Damaraland. "To this day Sir...no-one really knows." It is suddenly cooler again, the end of another day. I shiver, and gaze across to the lights of Uis once again. That night was bitterly cold he said, "Later in the year than this Sir... much later... the exhausted young men, they are talking late this night... tales of hard times... of aching hearts, of missing their clan, their mothers, fathers, kids, all their brothers and sisters."

I imagine a cooking fire, their meat all finished, their stomachs finally full, the men laying close for comfort and warmth. Their meagre blankets are thin, clothes threadbare. Eventually they fall into a fitful sleep, one by one, by one. The fire blazes and crackles, the encircling bushes oddly claustro-phobic. Dark shadows flicker and creep, the smoke seeping in silent perfumed drifts.

Northwards there is the darkening, forever horizon, and I imagine their somewhere homeland. I stare down at my dusty feet, then at the surrounding ground; all around me at the bare mounds of dirt. I imagine the buried bones, of eleven unknown young men that chose this resting place over any other. They cook their meat on a fire of `Melkbos', finally bedding down and sleeping rough: eleven weary travellers desperately seeking work but knowing nothing of Uis; all killed by poison, the men's warming fire fuelled by the hacked clumps of these surrounding bushes, the most toxic in these parts and the families left grieving, knowing nothing of that dire night, left wondering at the disappearance of family kith and kin.

55

UNFINISHED BUSINESS – Normandy, France, 2018

"I have less and less time and more and more to say" – *Pablo Picasso*

We sit on the edge of the wharf, the paving stones cold, the coffee shops closed. I gaze behind us at rows of seaside apartments, the drab dollhouse facade a collage of browns and greys. The aroma of cooked shellfish has more than a hint of garlic and parsley, along with Bob's Camel cigarettes, while white gulls cry from secret ledges and gutters. My friend likes it here, the quiet giving him time to think. Bob would be a tall man, his slender frame bent when walking, head down with the weight of an unfair world, a tweed sports coat that hangs from sharp shoulders and stinks of stale cigarette smoke. He has an unruly mop of grey hair and the smoker's wheeze of an old-time journalist, the wrenching cough and the weary grey face of long boozy lunches and late-night deadlines. We don't catch up that often, but he looks worse each time I see him.

"Yeah, there's lots of stuff I'd like to do. Stuff I need to say, that needs saying." Bob gazes across at the yachts, floating on glass, the mirror reflections unbroken. "But I need to bloody-well get on with it, I know." His eyes narrow and his gaze drifts back to me. "Funny, how things have just caught up to me I reckon. One minute I'm a young journalist with a world of injustice that needs to be outed. Then suddenly… " He looks down at his feet. There's another round of coughs wracking Bob's emaciated frame as he shakes, attempting to light up another smoke. I frown and my friend shakes his head knowingly, his untidy grey fringe falling across one eye. He has two marriages behind him, and two families, in Coventry and Shepherds Bush… one all grownup, and one not. He smiles a wan, worn-out smile. "To be honest mate, I leave loose ends everywhere, don't know how the hell they put up with me." I give a sympathetic nod, but from where I'm sitting, it seems they did not.

These days Bob is very much on his own, living alone in France, his Brit newspaper totally 'modernised' with massive layoffs of experienced players like him. "They can't even write these days", he gasps with a sideways glance, "haha… in my humble opinion that is." He pulls a small round tin from his pocket, twists off the lid and tucks in the latest cigarette butt. "And the editorial support, well, it's just not there these days."

I ask him what's ahead, and he stares out across the harbour, the gaggle of boats still adrift, languid and lazy. Bob shrugs. "There's a book in me I reckon. I've met some characters over the years." There is a half-hearted laugh.

I smile to myself at the thought of a man who worked and played hard, often at the expense of those around him and to the detriment of himself; known for not sleeping and endless drinking, a complicated soul with a social bent and a fierce intent to report injustice, undeserved privilege and political shams, who in the early days was infamous for returning late to his dingy office cubicle and crawling under his desk to sleep off the ubiquitous long lunches, then working frantically to midnight. That was until the ulcer, Bob eventually throwing up in a corner that passed for an office kitchen, then collapsing and waking under his desk the next morning, his crumpled white shirt a mosaic of splattered blood and vomit.

These days though, Bob often mentions 'time', me prone to reminding him of his 'book', and the ticking clock. It is always the same. He'll brush the hair from his eyes and tap the side of his head. "All up here mate", he says, "and that's the bloody hard bit done, for sure." But Bob catches my drift. "Yeah, yeah… I know. I'm just about to get started." He exhales another cloud of smoke and coughs again, a ragtag family fishing boat spluttering, the ancient motor leaving a black burned-out stench, the French tricolour flaccid, hanging from a crooked post aft, the grimy wooden hull smeared with pink paint primer.

I'm not sure if we really need to know how much time we have.

56

WAITING AT THE STATION – Tokyo, Japan, 2013

Standing at the Hachiko entrance to Tokyo's Shibuya Station, I ask about this dog on a pedestal, passed by over 700,000 commuters each day; the story beginning in 1924 with a rare pure-bred Akita dog arriving in Tokyo. His owner is a university professor, the dog seeing him off each morning and meeting him again each night at nearby Shibuya Station, rain, hail or shine. The following year his owner suffers a cerebral haemorrhage and dies at the university. That night the dog waits at the station. The dog's name is Hachiko, and he's given away after his owner's death, but routinely escapes and returns to his previous home, with his professor master never there. The dog walks to the station and waits.

Hachiko continues to keep vigil at the station every night at precisely the same time, searching among the faces of thousands of commuters for his master: the dog becoming a permanent fixture, fed by doting commuters who know the story. On March 8th 1935, Hachiko is found dead on a street nearby, finally succumbing to terminal cancer and a filaria infection.

I rub my hand over the nose of the dog's likeness; this the very spot where the pining pet kept vigil for 9-years after his owner's death, the now famous Akita dog still waiting for the return of his long-gone owner.

57

WANDERING WAYS – Skeleton Coast, Namibia, 2013

There is another white dual cab propped on the wrong side of the road. I wind down the passenger's window to ask if all is OK. A khaki-clad man pauses, narrow-eyed and hesitant way out here, water bottle pulled from an open, dust-laden tailgate. We are in Namibia, previously German South-West Africa, with the Namib Desert straddling the entire 2000km western coast but never more than 200km wide.

"*Ja*, the oldest desert in the world". Karl's a geologist, and nods his hatted head, the only other soul we've seen today. "For sure, this is true, there are not too many coming this way." He's slammed the fridge shut and tucked the bottle in a bulging side pocket, his sleeveless jacket the type favoured by well-off German tourists here; vest pockets full of pens and battered notebook, the back of those hands red from a searing yellow sun. He is interested in only "basalt", raising those bushy grey eyebrows. "*Ja*... and maybe the possibility of diamonds," having spent a lifetime in Damaraland mountains he "is knowing better than the Black Forest."

There's a bemused look on that sunburned face, the geologist shaking his head. "But you... you are going where?" Karl grimaces while pondering the thought. "You say... for 3-nights?" Silence again, him seeing no obvious sense in going "to a ruined diamond mine where there is nothing... nothing, but the winds, the wet and the cold."

I look past the geologist, to a flat and looming redness, then back to a worn moonscape skyline, and our distant dust trail that somehow hangs in limbo. The words "wet and cold" some alien notion, all around an engulfing, sweltering silence; the only obvious living thing, an occasional 2000 year old oddity of a prehistoric plant with two lonely leaves invariably shredded by Namib dust devils.

The air conditioning hums, Karl's dual cab just a speck in the rear-view, endless straight ahead, daunting hot and harsh: Spartan but sublime. How much difference could another 80km to the coast possibly make? Desert flats are sand, and scattered dolomite pebbles polished black by wind-born grit; way ahead a floating mirage, the imaginings of distant shimmering dunes shrouding a somewhere shoreline.

At the coast the sky has turned grey: a faded waterless wash, the road morphing to curves that blend and drift; some strange nether-land not sand nor sea. At Terrace Bay we finally stop, wash off dust, don jackets and bathe in cool sunset air while sitting on a raised concrete porch drinking hot mugs of rooibis tea. The sun is long gone, the sky still grey, the horizon too, the incessant boom on a steep beach, pounded by constant crashing waves.

Morning sees giant concrete pylons emerge from mist, once supporting a giant pipe with water for washing precious stones: what is left of an Onassis diamond mine; these 10m towers the skyscraper homes to black cormorant clusters, safe from wild Atlantic seas. Beady eyes stare, snake-like necks craning to take in our every move, our boots slipping on wet rocks and black, broken kelp. It's not difficult to imagine past hardships here, the failed dreams and lost lives, the bones of forgotten mines and over one hundred ships that litter a desolate coast: beached skeletons the wrecks of stranded wooden whales, casualties of an eerie phantom mist.

I turn my back to the Atlantic, and the cold air of a freezing Humbolt current, gazing east to the dunes, imagining shipwrecked sailors and the certain ordeal of trudging lost through endless dunes to perish in the Namib furnace from where we've come.

In the restaurant, I dine on tender oryx steak; my girlfriend, on linguini and garlic mussels, while the mechanic fixes our shredded tyre. The maitre'd wears a crisp white shirt and cowboy boots, restaurant walls covered with graffitied comments of adventurers from around the world; the wine a perfumed Stellenbosch Pinotage, the music Marley, Phil Collins and UB-40.

At the work shed, Josh is impressed at anyone driving

all day from the giant Etosha salt pan up north. "And you saw lions?" It is late, with Josh now under the bonnet of a Mercedes truck as I relate an encounter with two lionesses refusing to move from the road in front of our car. He shakes his head. In the morning we're leaving, and I am back at the work shed, having remembered the tank being almost empty. Josh clicks the pump into action and looks up. "You know, there is a lion that visits us here." I'm taken aback, not sure what to make of the now talkative Josh and the unexpected disclosure. I look around: the desolation and giant dunes, the great Atlantic sweep. Josh takes my point and smiles.

"A lone male tagged with a radio collar." Josh leans against our dual cab, balancing the pump in the crook of his arm. "Yes, he sometimes comes by. But we get little warning. It is kept a secret until the rangers, they ring us. He visits local waterholes. You would have certainly passed them when coming here." Water holes here? I make a mental note. The Terrace Bay bowser rattles and churns, Josh wide-eyed now. "This lion, he is special, his land stretching north 500km, all the way to Angola. This one, he swims the Kunene River."

Josh left the capital of Windhoek when still a kid; having high hopes of studying zoology in Johannesburg. There is a wan smile on that black face. He did time in the mines and drifted to odd jobs and truck repairs. "I arrive still young, and I hear of these desert lions. At first, like you, I say no way. But yes, he is roaming the beaches, looking for washed-up whales, seals and sometimes... he will take an oryx." I have seen oryx up north; the country's emblematic second largest antelope and a living cave painting; a dangerous option for a lion, being sometimes impaled on those sharp spear-like horns. But it seems there are other dangers for a lion.

The tank is finally full, Josh dropping the nozzle on the rusted bowser bracket but happy to continue the tale. "It is so interesting, this story of the lions." He suddenly stops, and I assure him I am listening. There is a flashing white grin before he goes on. "Before that time, when I arrive in 2002, there had been no lions here for over 10-years!" I must look doubtful, but Josh is insistent. "Yes, it is sad, but there had been trouble with the local people. They are so poor, with not so much food; kids and old people, few cows and goats." Josh nods. "There are problems with lions."

Even more recently, there had been one animal, collared like Josh's lion, but killed by a trophy hunter; then another shot shortly after, the fate of that small desert pride sealed with the death of the remaining two: sisters poisoned with strychnine. Josh looks up into surrounding dunes. "But this lion, he is still with us... somewhere."

Crashing waves drown the whirr of a distant helicopter: a silent north-bound speck high above, heading for a newly-built airstrip; the frontline in the Namibian search for oil and offshore gas. "We are a small nation of only two million... so we need this. It is for the future." Josh's voice lacks conviction. I sympathise, my thoughts too with his lion. We both stare north along a mist-bound coast. "Always alone that one." There's a wave of Josh's hand. "He travels up and down the coast; all this his kingdom."

Heading south we see the waterholes just off the road; secret reed-bound, oasis oddities and patches of parched grass; Atlantic to the west, endless dunes to the north, south and east. Flamingos stand on shining pink ponds: spindly stilted legs among silent mirrored brethren. Not 20m from where we stand, an oryx drinks, raising painted head to stare, rapier-sharp horns held high, sniffs the air and heads off, slowly turning for one last look from atop a dune. Today the king is nowhere to be seen.

58

WAYS OF THE WORLD – Beirut, Lebanon, 2015

Mirko is a bright-eyed 5 year old, peaked cap pulled backwards, in red Tee and baggy blue pants. I am taking in the balmy rays of a warm, dying sun that sinks in the horizon-hanging clouds of Beirut harbour. He has noticed my book sitting open on the bench. I ask him if he knows the writer. "But of course, it is Khalil Gibran," he nods. "Mama reads me the stories." His mother laughs. They are here most afternoons it seems.

Mirko tugs at his twin sister's sleeve, and I ask is she is a good sister. He looks at his mother, then back at me and screws up his nose. There is a smile and raised eyebrows from his mother. Does he like the water? Mirko is quiet for a moment, looks across to his mother and puffs out his chest. "But of course, we are the first to build the boats and sail on the sea." He knows the stories of his Phoenician ancestors, peers out to sea and informs me he can smell rain. I am impressed, and he swaggers off to join his sister.

His mother's name is Fayruz, a local teacher, and we sit staring out over a shining sea past chatting kids hanging on the balustrade. She worries about the future and shakes her head. "We hope for the best, and things are good. But they have not always been so." I close the pages of my book and Fay shrugs. Her eyes are glued to her kids. "You know, I try to be positive... to talk of achievements. They live in their own world right now and need time to be kids." She fiddles with the leather strap of her bag. "He will see soon enough the ways of the world."

Restless white gulls swoop low over the water and I watch as Mirka teases his sister. He knows of `The Prophet', the early sailors and the here and now; fun times with his cousins, his mother's stories, balmy coastal breezes and golden sun- sets. He speaks Arabic, French and English. He cares nothing for oil costs, climate change, religious fundamentalism, greed, hunger, or the unfortunate lot of the dispossessed.

59

WHERE THERE BE DRAGONS – Kadavu, Fiji, 2012

A courageous rooster crows in the sleepy Fijian village below. I clamber up concrete stairs by the dining room, along a spur straddling huts of palm frond thatch and sheets of rusted iron. Monster mango trees throw a shroud of welcome shade, cool and dark, over ragamuffin fence posts and loose strands of random wire. Motley chickens scratch. Spirals of smoke rise from cooking fires to a lazy sky of Fiji blue.

On the highest knoll I sit by a wind-bent palm sun on my back, gazing across at Nabukulevu; an extinct cloud-topped volcano with the incongruous sometimes-name of 'Mt Washington'. The expanse of the Great Astrolabe Reef stretches northwards towards Suva. There are wafts of smoke, the air smelling of burnt grass. Far below, a canoe-back yacht sits, shining white hull and masts aglow on early-morning indigo seas; the unsighted captain apparently choosing last night's tide to navigate these reef-strewn islands in total darkness. Ethereal bouts of Sunday singing drift on warm air; melodious melded voices rise and fall. The hair stands on the back of my neck.

After dinner we are joined at the beachside bar by the mystery captain; a lone Brit sailor making his way around the world. Robert is a retired London Doctor, having always wanted to sail. With the death of his long-time wife, he bought the yacht and took lessons, leaving Bristol to see the world. With the wryest smile, he relates his first adventure; alone and stranded on Spanish sandbanks. Robert could never go back. "There's nothing for me these days." For a moment his eyes are clouded and he turns away, musing over a glass of my Victorian Shiraz. And why Fiji? Robert shrugs. "Why ever not?" he answers. After sunset we fall quiet and wait for the mandatory green flash on the Kadavu horizon.

In the morning I walk barefoot along the village promenade, the sandy beach wide, the waves a mere murmur; the parking lot a gaggle of runabout tinnies. There are no roads here. Kids approach and pass, laughing eyes and white-teeth; proud and village-bound with bounty. They lug coconuts and breadfruit, hefty machetes swung from tiny hands. Generic tribes of dogs trot alongside; all tan with white-tipped curly tails and fox noses. I continue on, past the pigs and vegetable paddocks. In the shade the sand is wet – the smells organic here – the legacy of a Camelot downpour overnight. Twisted palm trunks curve wherever they will, while broken coconut shells peek from dank primeval layers of leaf litter, wrecked branches and discarded palm fronds. Cliffs hide behind, rising to the hot sun and grassy hills where I sat and pondered the arrival of Robert the morning before. Up ahead the boat sits just offshore, Robert's unruly mop of grey hair prominent as he busies himself with chores about the deck and sails.

I sit and watch from my secret haven, cold sand between my toes. His boat turns slowly one way, then again into the wind; sails flap gently then fill. Robert stands straight and peers ahead, one hand on the helm, the other brushing the fringe from his face. The boat slowly moves, leaving a wake of broken glass, the splosh of the bow breaking the spell. I wonder where he is headed.

60

A WHITE CHRISTMAS IN BLACK AFRICA – Lagos, Nigeria, 2014

I have been stuck in Johannesburg traffic for an hour now; finally pulling off the treadmill of Rivonia Rd, and into the Nigerian Consulate compound, open Tuesday and Thursday mornings only, then greeted by a mountain of a security man casually swinging a semi-automatic and demanding I stop. "You cannot be bringing your car in here, and must certainly be parking outside." The voice is classic Nigerian: all gravel and English gravitas.

I poke my head out the window and twist in my seat to peer back over my shoulder and from where I have come;

now a stationary stream of morning peak hour traffic. There is surely nowhere to park out there: the road so narrow, one lane each way, an insignificant uneven footpath propped on a high concrete kerb. There is a nonplussed shrug of those great shoulders. "Ahhh," he offers, "you must be improvising."

Thirty minutes later I am risking life and limb to veer clear of a gaping stormwater drain and pull to one side, mounting the kerb with a sickening crunch of the hire car underparts. The security guard nods as I pass; happier now as he swings his gun from one hand to the other, those black hands the size of plates and me shuffling a mass of paperwork in a green plastic folder. Inside I wait, surrounded by fellow would-be travellers that prefer to shout rather than quiet conversation. By the time I reach the counter, there's little time left. "A visa?" There's a serious frown happening behind that glass panel, "You applied on line?" I answer yes but am greeted by a sigh; a copy of my printed receipt turned around, then on its side for better inspection. I am already prepared for the worst but am taken aback by a startling white smile. "But you are lucky Sir, for we do have another form, and shall be most happy to see you again next week."

When leaving, my security friend waves with one hand, gun hanging loosely in the other. I again bemoan the Jo'burg traffic, and my chances of being in Lagos by Christmas. It's October already. There's a frown as he listens, and that now familiar African shrug. He leans close. "Traffic? Here?" He turns, following my gaze to the bedlam outside. "As you are travelling to Nigeria Sir, I'm thinking you must learn to be an optimist."

Now it's Christmas Eve, and here I am with my girlfriend in Lagos: the fastest growing, most vibrant and populace city in Africa; Nigeria a booming country of one hundred and seventy million. A battered, belching, clapped-out minibus lurches at 90degC just in front, having come from the complete opposite direction, crossing the bump of a median strip, on this flooded, potholed river of a road. A cavalier conductor wears purple tennis shoes and green shorts, propped precariously on one leg from what is left of a rear bumper. The other leg hangs clear. He waves with his free hand, spruiking fares as he goes, a shrill tin whistle poking from the corner of his mouth. I wonder how he stays on.

"Lagos traffic? Not so bad Sir," says Innocent; a recent City ruling banning motorcycle taxis, but resulting in an explosion of yellow tuk-tuks reminiscent of an extended stay in Mumbai. And it's my visit to that city, also of 20-million souls and making all this oddly familiar. Innocent is our driver, slightly built: a "good Christian man" with a wife and 3-kids. Innocent is surprised when I ask if he'll work on Christmas Day. "But of course Sir; there is no food for lazy man." The music of National treasure Fela Kuti blares from a boom box on the passenger's seat up front, Innocent's car radio broken.

From a palm-lined sandy peninsula beach we head for Lekki Market, more flooded roads, busted speed humps and countless corrugations: a beat-up car on a forlorn corner, a water-filled coke bottle on top – a sign this car is for sale. Narrow market aisles are lined with ramshackle and rusted lean-tos, rickety trestles loaded with exotic African wares, the darkest carvings and masks, paintings and woven placemats; wooden planks with piles of potatoes, pumpkins and plantains. The smells are earthen, humid and dusty. A cluttered shed of a bottle-shop sells Chivas, local Star beer, and boxes of South African wine.

I am reminded of a Jo'burg local, when I first broached the subject of me moving to Lagos: him calling Southern Africa "Africa Lite." I studied Johan's face closely, but this man gives nothing away. Finally, he cleared his throat, pursing his lips and shaking his head. "You are really going? Mmmm... now... *that* is Black Africa."

So, it is finally Christmas Day and we sit gazing out the window, our visit coinciding with the arrival of Harmattan winds, a seasonal visitor here, dumping tonnes of Saharan sand on Western Africa and shrouding Lagos suburbs in a thick white Christmas fog. The omnipresent generator kicks in just outside, a voracious city's power supply often failing. There's the crow of a brave Christmas rooster and the enticing aroma of roast chicken and thyme from the kitchen. We share a bottle of Moet Imperial Rose.

Innocent's open Christmas card sits on a wonky rosewood coffee table. "Heavenly Blessings shall be poured on you and your family. If there is anyone who plans evil against you and your family members, the evil shall go back to the sender... Amen."

61

WINDS OF WAR –
New York, USA, 2014

To the west, lay a somehow insignificant cityscape: the stacked steel and glass profile of a floating Manhattan. We wander among 7700 tonnes of precision-cut gleaming white stone taken from 12,100 tonnes of quarried granite: an architect's melding of modern imagination and ancient form, the 1.5-hectare Franklin D Roosevelt Four Freedoms Park. I am reminded of the bridge of a great white battleship. Roosevelt's 1933 bronze bust stares into a cold wind straight off the North Atlantic. The bust sits in a three-sided alcove on a raised table of solid granite; the walls 4m tall. At half a tonne and 70cm high, the bust is larger than life.

Initially known as `Blackwell', then `Welfare Island', this island was finally advocated – by a 1970 New York Times editorial – as a fitting site for a monument to Roosevelt. The

3km-long by 240m-wide island was renamed yet again in 1973; the architect, Estonian-born Louis I Kahn, presenting his ambitious vision for a memorial to a president he revered.

I first heard of this place back in East Village. "Hey, what you got on today?" demanded Cam, an architecture student from Colorado and the owner of our gentrified studio apartment. "There's somethin' you just gotta see, man," he pleaded. "A cool piece of work." He was praising Four Freedoms Park, pulling a booklet from a cluttered kitchen shelf and slapping it down on the table. "You are sooo lucky, dude, this park has only been open since October!"

It was Franklin Roosevelt who addressed US Congress in 1941, alerting the country to the threat of Nazi world domination and the necessity for war, passionately appealing to Americans' belief in freedom. Cam, less than half my age, reminded me that Roosevelt was struck down with infantile paralysis at age 39, was elected President four times and led the USA through the Great Depression and WW2. To reinforce his point, our young landlord took a faded cutting from a battered folder: a black-and-white picture of a suited and hatted man reading a newspaper while standing by a store on the corner of West 40th Street. The caption carried dire news from across the Atlantic. 'Nazi Army Now Seventy Miles from Paris – May 18, 1940'. That night, with Cam out partying, I shared a bottle of his cognac with my girlfriend, absorbed by the Four Freedoms story.

It is winter and we have checked out the New York weather forecast, taking Cam's advice and heading for the subway next morning. Alighting at the Island, we've walked south along the Manhattan side of the East River shore-line, a paved path edged by bare trees and park seats, under Queensboro Bridge and past the Coler-Goldwater Hospital. We have come to a gate in a black iron picket fence, passing the stone walled ruins of a smallpox hospital; a reminder of the island's past life, and a soon to be visitor centre.

The park entrance rises like a Mayan pyramid – a wide flight of pale granite stairs – at its foot a row of five copper-beech trees aligned with the stone ruins. At the top is a raised plaza enclosed in a low granite wall. It is an elongated triangle, with a central panel of lawn and surrounding paths of 261,000 cobblestones. Kahn's grand funnel design has directed our line of sight between the paved avenues of one hundred and twenty little leaf linden trees to the intended focal point, the bust of Franklin Delano Roosevelt.

New York City purchased the island in 1928. The road to the completion of Four Freedoms Park was tortuous, with a 99yr lease approved forty years later. A Kahn model was delivered to New York in 1974. The next year the project was put on hold due to a city budget crisis. Congress finally passed a bill to proceed with Kahn's plans in 1981 and basic site clearing and compaction commenced in 1994.

Kahn gleaned inspiration from the ruins of ancient Greece, Italy and Egypt; monumental, monolithic, bold and obvious. He knew great monuments take time; explaining in 1973: "I had this thought that a memorial should be a Room and a Garden... the garden a gathering of nature. And the room was the beginning of architecture... an extension of self."

I walk around Roosevelt's bronze bust. On the back wall, the President's fateful words include his base demands:

freedom of speech and expression, freedom of worship, freedom from want and freedom from fear. The text is bold V-cut letters, the words made even more dramatic, if that is possible, by the contractors having cut the text by hand; and the fact that if Kahn's project had gone ahead as planned in the 70s, the work would have been undertaken by the actual stonemason's father.

Now we are inside Kahn's 'room', my back to Roosevelt's words, the rectangular space defined by block walls to the east and west, but open to the sky. Steps lead down to a ha-ha with a low wall to the south; no railing to restrict the view. At the top of the steps we're on the southern tip of the island, the United Nations Headquarters sits to the west, over on the Midtown shore. A tug pushes a barge, skirting Manhattan docks and heading downtown. I wait for the sound of the wash against the wall where it drops into the darker grey of the East River.

Ambling back on the east side of the island we gaze across at Long Island City. By now it's late afternoon. We take the aerial tramway from Roosevelt Island in the shadow of Queensboro bridge, across East River to Uptown Manhattan. The tramcar finally approaches the docking station, both of us pondering the fate of Louis Kahn. He was never to see his Four Freedoms Park even begun, having died back in 1974; collapsing of a heart attack in the restroom of a New York train station, his body unidentified for three days due to a crossed-out address on his passport.

References

All text Copyright © Ian Cochrane 2022

National Library of Australia Cataloguing-in-Publication data: Cochrane, Ian James, 1951

Everything under the Sun – Australian short stories of light and shade from A to Z / Ian Cochrane, 2nd edition p-book, 6th edition e-book

Subjects:

    Cochrane, Ian James, 1951

    Adventure

    People

    Places

    Short stories

    The human condition

    Travel – Africa

    Travel – The Americas

    Travel – Asia

    Travel – Europe

    Travel – Oceania

    Travel – World

Cover image:'A World Away' Copyright © Ian Cochrane 2022